UNFORTUNATELY, A MIRACULOUS CURE

I can hear something being torn, then crumpled. He turns around, and he comes at me, Mr. Fink does, with something that looks like a wet napkin. And it smells like rubbing alcohol. "I think I should just keep them covered," I say, stuffing my hands behind my back.

"This won't hurt," he tells me. "I just have an idea that might help." Then he asks me for my hand, and when I finally give it over, he gently rubs my one wart until the whole thing comes off on the wet napkin.

"This isn't helping so much," I say.

When the wart is gone from my hand, all he says is, "Interesting."

I tell him that it is very interesting. *Very* interesting, making a big deal out of the "very." Because what else do you say to someone who knows you're a big fake and ruins your chances of not having to square-dance with Lippy Gordon?

OTHER BOOKS YOU MAY ENJOY

Double Fudge	Judy Blume
Fudge-a-Mania	Judy Blume
Matilda	Roald Dahl
Notes from a Liar and Her Dog	Gennifer Choldenko
Otherwise Known as Sheila the Great	Judy Blume
Penelope Crumb	Shawn K. Stout
Penelope Crumb Finds Her Luck	Shawn K. Stout
Penelope Crumb Never Forgets	Shawn K. Stout
Remarkable	Lizzie K. Foley
Savvy	Ingrid Law
Superfudge	Judy Blume
Tales of a Fourth Grade Nothing	Judy Blume
Ten	Lauren Myracle

PENELOPE CRUMB IS MAD AT THE MOON

SHAWN K. STOUT

with art by VALERIA DOCAMPO

PUFFIN BOOKS

PUFFIN BOOKS
An imprint of Penguin Random House LLC
375 Hudson Street
New York, New York 10014

First published in the United States of America by Philomel Books,
an imprint of Penguin Young Readers Group, 2014
Published by Puffin Books, an imprint of Penguin Random House LLC, 2015

THE LIBRARY OF CONGRESS HAS CATALOGED THE PHILOMEL EDITION AS FOLLOWS:
Stout, Shawn K.
Penelope Crumb is mad at the moon / Shawn Stout ; with art by Valeria Docampo.
pages cm
Summary: "Penelope Crumb makes a new friend when she is forced to learn how to
square dance at school"—Provided by publisher.
ISBN 978-0-399-16255-8 (hardcover)
[1. Square dancing—Fiction. 2. Friendship—Fiction. 3. Schools—Fiction.] I. Docampo, Valeria,
1976– illustrator. II. Title.
PZ7.S88838Pef 2014
[Fic]—dc23
2013030236

Puffin Books ISBN 978-0-14-242638-8

Printed in the United States of America

1 3 5 7 9 10 8 6 4 2

For the other side of the moon

1.

Today I am an elephant. In a costume that I made all by myself out of my mom's old gray sweat suit stuffed with pillows because it's Be an Animal Day at school. I painted a lion on the back of the shirt because when you're in the fourth grade you never know what's going to leap out at you from behind the bushes.

As I put on my paper-towel-tube elephant nose, plump my ears, and paint my hair and face gray, I think how nice it is to be something else in the mirror for a change. When my mom pokes her head in my room and tells me I'm going to be late and asks what's the deal with the lion, I say, "Portwaller Elementary can be a real jungle."

Walking to school from our apartment is only a couple of blocks, but when you're an elephant, for some reason, it seems to take a long time to get there. Plus there's all the strange looks you get on the way. The kind of looks that say Do You Know What You Look Like? I just smile at them in a way that means Yes Indeed I Am Supposed to Look This Way, I've Done So on Purpose And Not by Accident. More than a couple of people shout at me and offer me peanuts, but I just pretend they are the strange ones. I'm an excellent pretender.

But when I finally get to Portwaller Elementary, I know something is wrong as soon as I step inside: I'm the only animal at the zoo.

All of the other kids, and I mean ALL of them, are in normal, everyday school kind of clothes without a single tail or paw or beak. I start to elephant-sweat as everybody begins to stare at me, and when I wipe my forehead, some of the gray paint comes off on my fingers. Good gravy.

I see my used-to-be-best-friend, Patsy Cline Roberta Watson, at the drinking fountain. We're still friends, just not best ones anymore, mostly because of a girl called Vera Bogg who doesn't wear anything but pink. Which is something I will never understand.

When I go up to Patsy Cline, my elephant nose brushes against her hair and she screams and spits water all down her shirt. I tell her it's me, it's me, Penelope Crumb, but her shirt is already soaked and she's got a look on her face that says Don't You Know I'm Allergic to Things with Tails?

"Why aren't you dressed like an animal?" I say.

Then she says, "The real question is why are you?"

And when I remind her about Be an Animal Day, she shakes her head at me and says this: "You've got the date wrong, Penelope. It's two Mondays from now. And did you paint your hair?"

"No, it's today," I tell her.

"I'm sure that it's not," she says.

"No," I say, "today." Because it is. It has to be.

Patsy Cline turns me around by the shoulders so I can see all the kids without tails, and then she says: "Do you see anyone else that looks like you?"

This is a trick question, of course, because even if I wasn't dressed like an elephant I wouldn't see anybody that looks like me. I wouldn't. For one thing, my big nose.

Even so, as I look at everybody else, I see that Patsy Cline has a point. Good gravy, I'm the only elephant in the room.

I take off my elephant nose and look down at the rest of me. Gray, wrinkly, pillowy. I tell Patsy Cline that it could be worse, that I was thinking about being an ostrich, but then she points to my face and says, "What are you going to do about that? And your . . ."

But before she can finish, the bell rings and we're supposed to be in Miss Stunkel's classroom. "Come on," she says, pulling at my sleeve, "we're going to get hollered at."

But hollering isn't what worries me. It's showing up in Miss Stunkel's class all gray in the face and elephanty on a Regular Day and Miss Stunkel will say that I'm Quite the Riotous Disruption and send another note home. I'm pretty sure.

Patsy Cline doesn't want to help, I can tell. But I'm still holding on to her arm, and I guess she figures she doesn't have much choice, seeing how I'm not letting go, so she pushes down the handle to the water fountain and shoves my head into the stream. "Wash it off quick," she tells me.

I splash the water on my face and scrub with my hands until I see the gray paint begin to pool around the drain. Then I lift out my drippy head, keeping my eyes shut. "Did I get it off?"

"Some of it," says Patsy Cline. "But there's a good bit left. You need some soap. And a scrub brush. And there's no time to get you to the bathroom."

"I've got paint in my eyes," I say, after opening and then shutting them real fast.

"You need a towel."

I lean in toward her so she can dry my face, but I'm still drippy when she says, "I don't have a towel. Why would I have a towel?"

So, I have no choice but to take one of the pillows from my shirt and wipe my face with it. And when I'm done, Patsy Cline looks me over and says, "Oh dear." Which is not what I was hoping for. Then she tells me we've got to go pronto and pulls me down the hall to Miss Stunkel's classroom.

When we get there, I wonder if there is ever a place an elephant can hide. If there is, it isn't in Miss Stunkel's classroom, because I can feel everybody's eyeballs on me, even Angus Meeker, who lives to get me in trouble.

Vera Bogg: "Why are you dressed like a fat chimney sweep?"

Angus Meeker: "This is going to be good."

Patsy Cline: "It's just a mix-up. She's an elephant. Chimney sweeps don't have tails. Show her your tail, Penelope."

Me: "Patsy Cline, you are not helping."

All the while, Miss Stunkel is watching me from the front of the room while she pets the Monday lizard pin that hangs from her sweater. But to my surprise, she doesn't say anything to me about my painted face or hair, my stained and wrinkly gray sweat suit, or my tail. Instead, she just says, "Penelope Crumb and Patsy Cline, you do know that when the bell rings I expect you to be in your seats?"

Me and Patsy Cline say that we do indeed and that we're awful sorry. And then Miss Stunkel tells us, not just me and Patsy Cline, but tells everybody, to open our science books so we can learn about the solar system. The solar system! Miss Stunkel's going to talk about planets and moons, thank lucky stars, and doesn't have a thing to say about Penelope Crumb, Riotous Disruptor.

I pull out my science book from my desk with a smile on my gray mess of a face, eager to hear about stardust or moon craters or whatever outer spaciness that Miss Stunkel wants to make us learn. But then, I get to wondering why it is that Miss Stunkel hasn't said anything about Elephant Me. It's not that I want her to, believe me. I don't. But because she hasn't, it starts me thinking: Why?

Miss Stunkel tells us to read the paragraph in our books called "Interesting Moon Factoids." After the diameter, mass, and average distance from Earth, there is one interesting factoid that gets my attention:

There is no dark side of the moon. Both sides of the moon get the same amount of sunlight, but only one side of the moon is ever visible from Earth.

Right away I get to thinking how it doesn't seem fair that we only get to see one side of the moon from here. There's more to the moon than just that one side, and what if it was having a bad day or got its Mondays mixed up and that's all that people could see and not any of the good stuff.

Miss Stunkel must be able to tell what I'm thinking somehow because she says, "Is there a problem, Penelope?"

I say, "Not really a problem, I guess. I was just wondering something."

"Let's hear it," she says.

I shake my head and look at everyone else, who is already looking back at me. "Well . . ."

"Come on now," Miss Stunkel says. "I'm sure we'd all like to hear."

Patsy Cline gives me a look that says I'm Sure You Should Keep Your Mouth Shut. But I can't help it, I have to know why Miss Stunkel hasn't said anything about me being an elephant. "Well, I was just wondering if you noticed that I'm not myself today."

Miss Stunkel says that as a matter of fact she did.

"Oh," I say.

"Is there something else, Penelope?"

"And I was also wondering," I say, "why you didn't say anything."

Patsy Cline puts her head on her desk.

Miss Stunkel takes a deep breath, and her eyeballs bounce up and down like she's trying to search her brains for just the right words. She starts to say something a couple of times but then stops herself. Finally, she says, "Let's just say that *this*," and then she waggles her finger at me, the one that looks like a boiled chicken leg dipped in nail polish, the one that has been known to cause night terrors, "whatever *this* is called, falls within what I have come to expect of you, Penelope Crumb."

I'm not sure what that means exactly, but it sounds pretty bad. And I wish that lion on the back of my shirt would wake up and show its teeth or something. But it doesn't.

2.

I wonder about what Miss Stunkel meant the rest of the morning and into the afternoon, and all the way to gym. I like gym okay except for the running, the tumbling, the parachute, the rope climbing, the chin lifts, the arm hangs, and the sit-ups. Oh, and the shot put and hurdles. And dodgeball. Mr. Sanders, our gym teacher, hardly ever yells but he's really good at making you feel awful if you don't look like you're trying. So, I do my best. I'm excellent at pretending to try.

Mr. Sanders looks at the clock on the wall and says, "We're just waiting on the fifth graders."

Fifth graders? is what I say to myself. This can't be good. Even Angus Meeker looks worried.

I quick rub my face into my sleeve and look at Patsy Cline. But she crinkles up her nose and shakes her head. It's not easy getting rid of an elephant.

Just then the fifth graders stroll in real slowly and with their shoulders slumped and their heads bent toward the ground. Because that is how fifth graders walk. They line up against the wall and just stare at the rest of us like we've been pumped in from Portwaller's Sewage Treatment Plant. (We visited there last week, and let me tell you, it stinks.)

I keep my gray face down. It's best not to make eye contact because you never know, they could decide they don't like you. Or worse, they could decide that they do. So I just stare at the laces on my sneakers and only glance up once in a while like I'm thinking hard about toothbrushes or pillboxes or spare ribs or anything that has nothing at all to do with them.

During one of my glance-ups I see Hugo Gordon, a fifth grader who is sort of on the big side, big all over really. Some people call him "Hugest," but most people call him "Lippy" on account of the beads of sweat that coat his top lip and make it shine. I don't know where all that sweat comes from or why it decides to hang out on his lip for everyone to see and make fun of, but it's always there. Always, always. You can see that shine from ten feet away or more, maybe twenty if the light is just right.

One time when I had to deliver a note to our principal's office, I saw Hugo up close. He was standing outside the principal's door for some reason, and I saw him. He wiped his lip with the back of his hand, and right after he did, that shine was back, sweat beading up all over the place. I only noticed because 1) I happened to be looking at his nose, which is regular-size but looks small probably because the rest of him is so big; and 2) it's an artist's job to notice things like sweaty lips. And I, Penelope Crumb, am going to be an artist when I get to be a grown-up.

"Do you all know why you're here together?" Mr. Sanders asks, picking up two cloth bags by the door, one purple and one green. He swings them in circles so the rope drawstrings wrap around his hands, and then he swings them the other way. "Because you lucky youngsters are going to learn square dancing. That's why."

Lots of people groan, but I'm the loudest, I'm pretty sure. Mr. Sanders tells us he doesn't want to hear it and that it will be a lot more fun if we start out with a better attitude. But when it comes to dancing, in a circle or square or anything else, my attitude doesn't get any better.

And then all of a sudden music starts playing from speakers on the wall. Music from the olden days when it was terrible and silly and when nobody knew any better. *"Swing your gal, round she goes, where she stops, nobody knows."* Mr. Sanders does a little shuffle with his bright white tennis shoes.

All the fifth graders laugh. I would laugh, too, if my brains weren't too busy worrying about what was in those bags.

But I don't have to worry for too long, because as soon as that awful song ends, Mr. Sanders holds up those bags and says, "What oh what do I have in here?" He reaches into one bag and pulls out a thin strip of paper. He's still shuffling. "I've got your dance cards, that's what," he answers himself. "I'm going to pull a name from each bag, and when I do, I want you to partner on up."

He clears his throat and reads the name on the slip of paper. "Margot Hill." Margot steps out of the fifth-grade lineup and makes her way over to Mr. Sanders, who is already reaching into the other bag. Margot's face has turned a pretty shade of Wild Strawberry and she's got her eyeballs turned up at the ceiling like she's praying for some sort of miracle or maybe a lightning bolt. Then Mr. Sanders says the next name: "Angus Meeker."

Angus Meeker takes a step forward, but only after Patsy Cline gives him a push between the shoulder blades with her thumb. "Quit," he tells her, but he won't go any farther.

One of the fifth-grade girls, I think her name is Nancy Jo, says, "We have to dance with *them*?" She means us.

"Do you?" Mr. Sanders asks. "It would appear

so," he answers. Then he tells Angus Meeker to step right up and that it's not polite to keep a young lady waiting. Angus Meeker eventually does step right up but he won't look at Margot Hill or anybody else. Margot Hill finally stops her praying and gets a look on her face that says My Life Is Over.

Panic sets in. And we all start scanning the room to see which one of us we don't want to be stuck with. And that's when I notice that a lot of the fifth graders are looking right at me. And I can tell, *I can*, that I, Penelope Crumb, am The One No One Wants to Dance With. I know the way you know your pants are too tight: It hurts.

Other than my big nose, I can't think of why I'm any more of The One than, say, Vera Bogg. I mean, if there's a The One among us it's Vera. Because for starters, all the pink she's always got on.

Then I look down to see what I've got on. And I remember that today I am an elephant.

Well then.

I scrub my face with my shirtsleeve, harder this

time, to try to show those fifth graders that it's only paint, that really, I'm not The One. I'm not. Believe me.

Meanwhile, Mr. Sanders continues to dig into his bags, and I stop de-elephanting long enough to hear the names. Soon, Patsy Cline and Vera Bogg are matched up and so is most everybody else. Those who already have partners don't seem quite as miserable as before because now they are already on the other side watching the poor souls who are left. And they are whispering and laughing at us.

That's when Mr. Sanders calls my name. I get to my feet, feeling the weight of an elephant and a lion on my back. The whispers get louder, especially from that fifth grader named Nancy Jo, who was just matched up before me. In fact, her whispers are so loud they don't even count as whispers anymore, seeing how I can hear them across the room. She says, "What is wrong with that girl?"

I am about to loud-whisper right back that not a thing is wrong with me, if she wants to know so bad, other than getting Mondays mixed up, which could happen to anybody. I am about to tell her this, but

Mr. Sanders tells everyone to put a lid on it and then pulls a name out of the green bag. As he does, I realize I'm saying to myself, inside my head, over and over, "Not Hugo Gordon. Not Hugo Gordon."

Because the only thing that will make them laugh more than Elephant Girl, is Elephant Girl partnered with a kid everyone calls Lippy.

I hold my breath, but it doesn't do any good because Mr. Sanders says the name of my square-dance partner. And when he does, all I can see is Hugo Gordon's shine.

3.

Littie Maple asks me if I want to go with her to Mueller's Drug Store down the block to get some candy.

"Your momma's still craving jelly beans?" I ask.

"Only the green ones," she says. "Momma says this baby is going to come out looking green because of all the green candy she's been eating. But I don't mind since she lets me eat all the other colors." Littie lives across the hall but lately spends more time in our apartment than hers. Because, for one thing, we have a TV. And for another, Littie's momma is going to have a baby and, according to

Littie, has a growing appreciation for peace and quiet.

"No, thanks, I'm busy," I tell her. "But I'll take any orange ones you don't want."

"Busy doing what?" she asks. Probably because I'm just sitting here on the front steps of our apartment building looking like I'm not doing anything at all. But just because somebody looks like they aren't doing anything doesn't mean they really aren't. They could be waiting for their mom to come home so she can write a note to get them out of square dancing. That's a lot of doing something.

I tell Littie this, and she says, "Square dancing sounds like fun."

"It's not," I say. "Believe me."

Littie looks like she's not so sure. But she's home-schooled, always has been, so it's not her fault if she doesn't know what's fun and what's not. "Teach me some steps," she says.

"I don't know any. We haven't actually done any dancing yet."

"Then how do you know it isn't fun?" she says.

"Because for one thing," I say, "it's dancing in front of people, and for another, it's dancing with a boy. And if you need another reason, Littie Maple, which I don't know why you would, it's because not only do you have to dance with a boy, you probably have to hold hands with him, too. Even worse, he probably has to hold hands with you."

She shrugs and gets a look on her face that says That's Not So Bad. Littie Maple is a year older than me, and all I can figure is that there must be some magic that happened in that year to make her not mind boys so much.

"You don't think your mom is really going to write a note for you, do you?" she says.

I nod. "Why not? She wrote a note for Terrible that time, after he got his tonsils out, and then he got out of going to his debate club tournament." This was before my older brother, Terrence, was abducted by aliens and returned as Terrible. Without any note at all.

"But you aren't having your tonsils out," she tells me. "I'm just saying."

I give her a look that says What Does That Have to Do with the Color of Mud? And then I say, "I know that. But the point of the story is the note, not the tonsils."

Littie says, "What excuse are you going to use for not dancing?"

I shrug. "I don't need an excuse. I just need a note." Then I explain to Littie how notes work. "A note from a parent can get you out of anything at school. If there's a note, teachers can't make you do anything. It's a rule."

She tells me good luck and then asks if I don't get a note will I teach her some square-dance steps. I tell her okay, but she shouldn't get her hopes up because there is no way I will be dancing in a square or any other shape.

After Littie leaves, I watch the people on our busy street, hoping that one of them will soon be my mom. And while I'm sitting here, I don't know why it happens, but I start to sing that awful song from gym class. *"Bow to your lady, bow to your gent, follow your lady left, that's the way she went. Into the center now, tall and grand, come back and promenade all around the land.*"

I don't even realize I'm doing it until Mrs. Mason from apartment 3B passes me on the steps and says, "Catchy little ditty, Penelope."

"Oh," I say. Because what else do you say when somebody catches you singing a song you don't even like and don't know you're singing and can't get out of your head? I tap my brains with my fingers to make the music stop. And it does, thank lucky stars, as soon as I see my mom and Terrible walking toward me.

"Oh, too bad, you took your elephant costume off already," Mom says.

"How can you tell?" says Terrible, showing me his alien teeth.

I ignore him. The thing about having an alien for a brother is that you can always count on him for a big-nose remark.

Mom says, "I wanted to take a picture of you and I forgot to do it this morning."

I tell her she will have another chance in a couple

of weeks, I suppose. When she looks at me funny, I tell her I had the wrong day.

Terrible pushes past us and heads up the stairs, right after whispering to me that I am such a dufus. I would say something back, I would, but now is not so good of a time for an alien fight. Besides, he's been in a mood lately, ever since that Tildy girl stopped calling him and coming over for dinner. Mom says that he's a teenager and just needs some space to work it out, and I tell her that there are a lot of miles between us and Jupiter so he better get going.

I hang back with Mom and let Terrible get way ahead. Then I say, "You know something, Mom? I think there are some things in school that just shouldn't be taught."

"Oh dear," she says, hiking her backpack on her shoulder.

"You know, I mean it's fine to do some things. But other things, definitely not. Like there should be a law against it or something."

"What are you talking about exactly?" says Mom.

"Dancing," I tell her.

"Dancing?" she says as we get to the top of the stairs.

"Yes, dancing."

"You want there to be a law against dancing?" she says. "Am I hearing you right?"

"Yes I do," I say. "Especially at school."

Mom unlocks the door to our apartment, and after we all go inside, she puts down her bag by the door, takes off her jacket, and says, "Miss Stunkel sent another note home, didn't she?"

"No," I say. "But speaking of notes." Then I tell her how I need her to write me one so that I don't have to square-dance in gym. I leave out the part about Hugo Gordon, about his sweaty lip, about everybody's whispers.

She says, "I thought you liked dancing."

I shake my head.

"Really? I thought for sure I saw somebody that looked exactly like you dancing around the living room just last week."

"Nope."

"And bouncing on the sofa and waving her arms."

My face gets warm. "Nope."

"And wiggling her bum."

"Mom. That never happened."

"My mistake, I guess."

"So will you write me a note?" I say.

Mom sifts through the mail on the hall table. "I don't think so." Then she holds up her hand at me and says, "And don't say that isn't fair."

I put a look on my face that says That's Not What I Was Going to Say Anyhow. Even though it very much kind of was. And then she tells me that a little square dancing won't kill me.

I say, "How do you know?" Because it just might.

"I *know*," she says. And then she gives me a look that means Now Don't You Go Start Talking About Dead Things.

But I can't help myself. I've got a dad who is Graveyard Dead, and when you have one of those, it's hard not to think about dead things once in a while. I say to Mom, "I bet you that somewhere sometime there was someone who died from square dancing. And you never know, the next time it happens could be me."

She says, "Penelope Rae," and the way she says it makes my name sound like one of the diseased body parts she draws for her job. Irritable bowel syndrome, for example. My mom's drawings are in books that doctors read. She goes to school, too, because you have to go to a special school to learn how to draw people's insides. But does she have to learn square dancing at her school?

She does not.

4.

ittie Maple is on our couch watching TV while I'm paging through one of Mom's insides books looking for diseases of the hand. There are so many gross ones to choose from, thank lucky stars. Osteoarthritis, Buerger's disease, Heberden's node, Bouchard's node. I look up from the book. "Hey, Littie, do you know what a node is?"

Littie keeps her eyes on the screen and says, "A small mass of tissue. You don't want one. Why?"

"Small mass of tissue," I repeat. "Something big would be better." I keep reading. "Dactylitis, ganglion cyst, gout. What about gout? That sounds pretty good."

Finally, when there's a commercial, Littie asks me what I'm going on about.

"I don't think I'll be able to square-dance with a bad case of the gout, do you?"

She shakes her head at me. "No note?"

"Mom says I have to dance, that it won't kill me, even though I'm pretty sure it will." I turn the page. "How about warts?"

"You don't have warts," says Littie. "I'm just saying."

I tell her I know I don't, but Mr. Sanders doesn't know that, and what if I put bandages all over my hands and fingers?

She says, "And your feet."

I smile and say, "Now you're thinking, Littie Maple."

"Too bad you're not Amish. They don't believe in dancing. It's against their religion."

"Some people are so lucky," I say. "How do you get to be Amish?"

Terrible walks through the living room just then

and tells me I can't be Amish, moron, and asks, "What are you, stupid?"

I tell him that this is none of his business, who is he to tell me I can't be Amish if I want to be, and by the way, would a stupid person work so hard to get out of square dancing in gym?

He seems to consider that for a moment before shrugging and then walking away. See, even aliens don't want to square-dance. This must be what is called a Universal Truth.

"What's wrong with him?" asks Littie.

I give her a look that says You Mean Besides Being an Alien? And then I tell her: "Girl trouble. And also he has the kind of problem that's called not being a human."

"Right," Littie says.

"So what do I have to do to get Amish?" I say.

"You don't *get* Amish. You just are or you aren't. And, anyway, I don't think you'd want to be Amish, Penelope. You'd have to move to the country and work in fields."

"I could do that."

"And give up TV," she says. "And you'd probably have to wear a dress all the time and a bonnet on your head."

"Oh," I say. "I don't really like to wear hats."

"Yeah," says Littie, "your ponytail would get in the way."

I look at my hands. "Warts it is, then."

At school, I press down the bandage strips on my hands, all nineteen of them, to make sure they stay on good. And I keep my hands on top of my desk so everybody can see. It works. Vera Bogg is the first to notice. "What's the matter with your hands?" She looks horrified.

"Warts," I tell her. And just for fun I say, "The contagious kind."

Patsy Cline inches her desk chair away from me. In addition to things with tails, Patsy Cline is also very much allergic to germs, and she wants to know right away how I came to get them and also what I'm doing to get rid of them.

"I don't know" is what I tell her, and also, "I guess

they just have to go away on their own." She doesn't like this answer, I can tell.

Angus Meeker says, "I didn't know there was such a thing as contagious warts. Let's see one."

I tell him fine, and I start to peel away one of the bandage strips. As I do, some other kids in Miss Stunkel's class gather around to have a look. I pull back the strip real slowly until the white-and-brown spot appears.

Angus Meeker: "Are you sure that's a wart?"

Patsy Cline: "You should probably cover it back up now, Penelope."

Vera Bogg: "Very, very disgusting."

Angus Meeker: "Let me see it again."

I show him again real quick and he says, "I don't think that's real. It doesn't look real to me."

Me: "It does, too. It looks just like the ones in my mom's book." I should know, because I spent all night painting each one.

If Mister Leonardo da Vinci was here (who happens to be my All-Time Favorite dead artist), he would surely say, "Pray tell, the last time I saw a pustule that authentic, oh me, oh my, was on the back of a warty toad." (Because that is how dead artists talk.)

Miss Stunkel must think so, too, because as soon as she gets a look at my bandaged-up hands, she asks me if I have a note from my doctor.

I wish.

I tell Miss Stunkel that notes are apparently harder than usual to get these days and that I'll be fine as long as I don't have to do anything that would require me to hold hands with anybody. Like dancing, for example.

Miss Stunkel gives me a look that says What Are You Up To, Girlie? And then she says just to be safe, why don't I go down to see the school nurse. Which is fine by me because I'd rather do anything than learn about decimal points. Except square-dance, of course.

It must be a slow sick day, because I don't have to wait long at all to see Mr. Fink (that's his name, for real). He's the school nurse. He tells me to come right in. Mr. Fink is tall and skinny with a long, flat nose that barely sticks out past his lips. "What seems to be the problem?" he asks me, eyeballing my hands.

"Warts," I say.

He tells me to sit down on a chair. "How long have you had these?"

"Not long," I tell him. "I just kind of got them."

"They just popped out overnight? I mean to say, you didn't have them yesterday?"

"Right. I didn't have them yesterday."

He sits on a stool and wheels himself over to me. "May I see one?"

He smells like disinfectant, and I can't help but notice how the light from the ceiling shines on his mostly bald head in the shape of a giraffe. I can almost hear that giraffe say, "Can we get some hair up here? I'd feel a lot better if there was some hair to hide behind."

I tell Mr. Fink okay and then he takes some gloves out of a box and puts them on. He pulls back one of my bandage strips and I watch him as he does. His eyebrows go up a little, and then down, and then up again. He pulls the bandage strip the whole way off and he's got a look on his face that says Very Suspicious.

"They are the contagious kind," I say, "so you don't want to get too close."

He says, "Humph" and then nothing else. He opens the door to the first aid cabinet on the wall. He's got his back to me, so I can't see what he takes out of there, and this makes me start to worry.

I can hear something being torn, then crumpled. He turns around, and he comes at me, Mr. Fink does, with something that looks like a wet napkin. And it smells like rubbing alcohol. "I think I should just keep them covered," I say, stuffing my hands behind my back.

"This won't hurt," he tells me. "I just have an idea that might help." Then he asks me for my hand, and when I finally give it over, he gently rubs my one wart until the whole thing comes off on the wet napkin.

"This isn't helping so much," I say.

When the wart is gone from my hand, all he says is, "Interesting."

I tell him that it is very interesting. *Very* interesting, making a big deal out of the "very." Because what else do you say to someone who knows you're a big fake and ruins your chances of not having to square-dance with Lippy Gordon?

Then Mr. Fink hands me the wet napkin and tells me to go on now and get rid of the rest of them and then I can get going back to class. But I don't want to get rid of them. When I tell him this, all he says is, "I'm sure you don't want me to write a note."

And I say, "Actually, Mr. Fink, it would be really great if you could."

5.

Mr. Fink sends me back to Miss Stunkel wart-less and without a note. He even takes all of my bandage strips away.

As soon as I get back, Miss Stunkel tells me to open my math book because the rest of the class that hasn't been in the sick room are just now starting a lesson on decimals and percentages. I don't see how things could get any worse until she looks at my hands and says, "Penelope Crumb, you seem to be cured. What a miracle."

A couple of people laugh and I can feel my face get hot. I sit down at my desk, and as I open my math book, Patsy Cline whispers, "What happened to, you know, those things on your hands?"

I shake my head at her.

She says, "Are they still contagious?"

Angus Meeker says to Patsy Cline and whoever else is listening besides me, "They weren't real. I told you they weren't. Didn't I tell you?"

I give Angus a look that says They Could've Been, You Don't Know.

Miss Stunkel holds out her chicken-bone finger at us and she tells us to get quiet right away or else.

Somehow I make it through math and the next three periods. But by the time we are supposed to line up for lunch, everybody wants to know where my warts went and how long before they come back.

In the cafeteria, word spreads like head lice. Kids I don't even know are asking to see my painted-on warts. "You shouldn't make fun of people with fake skin problems," I tell them, shoving my hands in my pockets. They want to look anyway, probably because a case of hand warts, real or not, could be the most interesting thing to happen at Portwaller Elementary the whole year. "Fine," I say, showing them my hands. But when they don't see even one wart, they droop and shake their heads at me like I've just robbed them of any chance for fun, and how could I do something so cruel?

I sit with Patsy Cline at lunch like regular, and every once in a while she looks over at me and my hands, probably to see if any germs are hopping off me in her direction. It's enough to make me not want to eat any of my apricot jelly sandwich. Which is really too bad because it's my favorite.

So here I am staring at my sandwich while Vera Bogg and Angus Meeker and Patsy Cline and everybody else at the table are going on about last night's episode of *Max Adventure*. And that's when I see Hugo Gordon sitting at a table all by himself. I watch him for a while, wondering how he doesn't seem to notice anybody else is around, or maybe he doesn't care that he's eating all by himself, and even if he does care, how he keeps his eyeballs on his plate. And how that lip is really coated with sweat.

Everybody else hardly seems to notice him. And

maybe that's a good thing because when they do, it isn't nice. Like when that girl Nancy Jo walks by and pushes another girl so that she bumps into Hugo right when he's drinking from his milk carton. The milk drips down his chin, and Nancy Jo laughs.

I watch him, I do, this whole time, and not once does he say anything to Nancy Jo or the other girl. Not "You should say you're sorry" or "Look where you're going, would you?" or "You owe me another milk." Nothing like that. He just sits there with milk dripping down his chin onto his shirt like bumping into him on purpose happens all the time. Like maybe he deserves it.

Just when I start to think that it must be the Worst Thing being Hugo Gordon, I find out that the entire fifth grade has heard about my fake warts. I find out because Patsy Cline tells me after lunch on the way to gym.

"They've got a name for you," she says, keeping a bit of a distance because, you know, germs and all.

I'm pretty sure I go dead right there, right in the

hallway. This happens to me sometimes, so I recognize the signs. My legs stop working, I can't feel my toenails, and I can see Patsy Cline's lips move, but I can't hear anything she's saying. This is what happens when your life is over on the way to gym where you will have to hold hands with Lippy Gordon and dance with him, in a square, even though you don't want to at all but have to anyway because you are not Amish.

The last thing you want to happen in fourth grade is to get a name from the fifth graders. Do you think Lippy Gordon has always been Lippy Gordon? He was just plain Hugo until last year when he was in fourth grade and the fifth graders started to notice him and his sweaty lip. Now he'll probably never be just regular Hugo again ever.

Patsy Cline nudges me in the arm with her elbow and says something else, but I don't know what. All I can think about is that the fifth graders have given me a name. One that I don't want, I'm pretty sure.

"What is it?" I say when I get alive again. "What's the name?"

Patsy Cline winces. Like she's the one that's been speared.

I give her a look that says You Might as Well Tell Me Because I'm Going to Find Out Eventually.

She sighs a really heavy sigh like she's sorry she's the one that has to deliver this rotten news. Then she says it. "Wartgirl."

6.

Wartgirl?" I say.

Patsy Cline nods.

"That's not very original." But I'm a little relieved because I was really expecting something that had to do with my big nose.

She shrugs. "Some people are saying 'Wannabe Wartgirl.' You know, since, I guess, they weren't real and all."

"Wannabe Wartgirl," I say, giving it a try. "That's a little better."

Patsy Cline says she's sorry again. And she kind of pats me on the shoulder but not really. The germs.

The rest of the way to the gym, my brains are thinking about one thing: Wartgirl. It's on my tongue, too. The name, I mean. Wartgirl. *Wannabe Wartgirl.* And I think that it's a really mean name for someone who has warts. But for someone who doesn't, like me for example, and who doesn't want them for real and was only just pretending to have warts for a very good reason, it's the kind of thing that's called Really Dumb. And I decide to tell that to the person who came up with it.

"Who said it?" I ask Patsy Cline when we sit on the bleachers in gym. "I'm thinking it's probably that Nancy Jo girl."

But before she can answer, Mr. Sanders starts talking. "Have I been hearing some complaints circulating about square dancing?" he says. "Yes, I have. Lots of complaints, actually. I can't say that I'm too surprised, I guess, but do I have an idea to help get you all in the right frame of mind about square dancing? Oh boy, do I." He wheels a television in front of us.

"We're going to watch TV?" asks some fifth grader.

Mr. Sanders smiles and says, "So glad you asked. As a matter of fact you are. And what you see I hope will change your attitude."

"Does this mean we don't have to do any dancing today?" I ask, sitting on my hands.

I hear some Wartgirl whispers from girls behind me, and when I turn around to see who it was, there's Hugo Gordon looking at me, right at me. He's two rows behind me and all the way at the end and there's nobody sitting near him. I turn around real quick.

"That's exactly the kind of frame of mind we need to change," says Mr. Sanders. "And I was going to save this for the end of class, but I might as well tell you now. Vice Principal Hardy and I were talking, and we're going to have a hoedown here, at the school, in a few weeks. We're going to invite the rest of the school to come and watch you dance, along with your families."

There's some moaning that happens then. A lot of it comes from me, I'm pretty sure.

Mr. Sanders says, "Did I mention that there's going to be a prize for the best group? No? Well, now I have. Squares will score points in several categories. Number one, synchronicity. That means swinging and turning at the same time. Number two, timing, you know, keeping in step with each other. Number three, dress attire. That means you should try to look nice. And finally, number four, which in my mind is the most important, attitude. Do you have to try to look like you are enjoying yourself? You most certainly do. Any questions?"

One of the fifth graders says, "What's the prize?"

"Oh, did I forget to mention that part?" asks Mr. Sanders. "I must've. The prize for the square with the most points is tickets to opening day of the new adventure park, which I believe is in Simmons." He taps the heel of his shoe on the floor. "What is the name of it? I think it's called . . ."

"Adventureland!" says Nancy Jo.

"Adventureland," he says. "Thank you, Nancy Jo. That is indeed what it is called."

In between lots of squeals, everybody is talking about the Adventureland roller coaster called Spin Rocket that is supposed to be one of the fastest ever.

So fast that you have to wear special goggles to protect your eyeballs from being sucked back into your head. And how they all want to be first in line.

Then Mr. Sanders tells us all to be quiet and turns the TV on. Before I know it, on the TV there are women in brightly colored wide skirts and funny hair piled on top of their heads and men with matching shirts on, some with ruffles down the front, and cowboy hats.

Everybody's already giggling, and the music hasn't even started yet. Mr. Sanders tells us, "For goodness' sakes, for once would you please keep an open mind?"

I'd like to open up my mind, I really would, but if I do, who knows what will fall into it. The dancing starts, and there's a man with a microphone on a stage and he's doing more talking than singing. Mr. Sanders says, "He's the Caller. Listen to what he's saying. He's telling the dancers what to do."

"Back to the center now, do-si-do, swing your partner and around you go."

I sneak a look at Hugo Gordon, and he's got his

eyeballs on the TV, watching, watching, watching. His lip is as sweaty as ever, and he must be really into watching those dancers because he doesn't even try to wipe it away.

"Ladies circle left and leave your man, back to the center as quick as you can."

Hugo Gordon's thumb is on his knee, tapping to those silly words and that awful music, and when I turn around again, to my surprise, I see my wartless thumb is doing the same thing.

7.

Those dancers are doing a lot of arm- and hand-holding, I notice. Too much, in fact. And I don't like it. I want to ask Mr. Sanders if we have to do that when we dance or can we just pretend to hold hands.

But before I have the chance to ask, the video is done, and Mr. Sanders takes his clipboard from under his arm and says the three words that I've been hoping never in my life to hear: "Let's square-dance!"

I guess finding out about the prize and watching those dancers on TV worked for some people just like Mr. Sanders wanted, because as soon as Mr. Sanders says these words, Patsy Cline and Vera Bogg and some other kids, boys even, jump up like they can't wait to swing their partners. But none of *them* have someone called Lippy for a partner. Maybe if I was partnered with someone else I wouldn't mind so much. I'm not sure. Maybe I would.

I can't look at Hugo Gordon, I can't, because all I can do is stare at my fingers, which are starting to get itchy and sweaty, and I'm wishing so hard that some warts would sprout right up.

They don't.

Mr. Sanders calls our names in groups of eight and tells us to stand next to our partners in squares on the gym floor. When I hear my name, I get to my feet, I don't know how because my toes are numb and stiff—a sure sign of being dead—and the next thing I know I'm standing in a square wondering if the rest of me goes dead right here will I still have to dance?

My square gets filled up quick. Vera Bogg is there, with her partner, but Patsy Cline is in another square, one over. Then comes some other fifth graders, including that awful Nancy Jo.

And soon after, Lippy, I mean, Hugo Gordon is standing right beside me. Nancy Jo gives him the Stink Eye, the kind that Terrible gives me when he's about to plant a knuckle punch in my arm. Then she says at him, "Oh no." And she makes a big deal out of the *no*. "Now we'll never win."

Hugo looks at his feet this whole time. Like maybe he's hoping they will just take charge and start running. I keep looking at his hand, the one that I'm going to have to hold with my own. And then all of a sudden I have to get my brains to think of something else besides holding hands because otherwise I will go dead for real. So I just start talking, talking about what I'm not sure exactly but I have to put words out there, for some reason, I have to. And these are the words that come out: "More people die from donkeys than plane crashes."

Hugo Gordon looks at me then, and Nancy Jo shoots her partner a look that says Why Is She Talking About Dead Donkeys?

"It's true," I say.

Mr. Sanders says, "Are we are going to go over

some calls? We are, indeed. Just the basics, folks. Now, when the Caller says 'circle left' you grab hands and go around to the left until you are back to where you started."

I look at Hugo's hand. His thumb is tapping his leg. I blurt out in a panic, "Coconuts kill more people than sharks."

"Coconuts?" says Vera Bogg. "But I like coconut."

Nancy Jo asks, "What did she just say?"

I think Nancy Jo is talking about me and not Vera, but it doesn't matter because Vera licks her lips and says, "Especially coconut and chocolate." Which makes Nancy Jo say something under her breath that I can't hear but am sure isn't nice.

"Okay," Mr. Sanders says, "let's give it a try. Join hands and circle left."

Vera Bogg and her partner hold hands, and then Nancy Jo and her partner, and then the two other fifth graders in our square. Vera Bogg's partner is on my left and he looks at my hand like he's maybe heard about the warts, but then he takes my hand in his. Kind of grabby-like, if you want to know the truth.

It's not so bad, though, this holding hands thing. I mean, it doesn't kill me, not yet anyway, so I glance over at Hugo, and his thumb has stopped tapping. I reach for his hand, the one closest to me, but it doesn't move.

Well then.

A fifth grader girl named Helena is on the other side of Hugo, and she's got her hand behind her back.

Mr. Sanders says, "People, do I need to come around to each square and show you how to hold hands? I don't think I do."

Hugo reaches out his hand in Helena's direction.

"Come on, Helena," says Nancy Jo, smiling, "hold hands with him. You have to."

Helena gives Nancy Jo a look that says You're Going to Get It, and then she takes his hand, but she's looking the other way the whole time, like she's sticking her hand in a rat hole and can't bear to watch her fingers get gnawed to stubs. Once they're holding hands, Helena gives out an "ew" sound and Nancy

Jo laughs, but I don't see what's so funny, because Hugo Gordon still isn't holding hands with me.

The next thing I know, Mr. Sanders is behind us telling me and Hugo that we better hold hands this instant. Which is the worst thing ever that could happen because 1) he says it kind of loud; and 2) now everybody is staring at me and wondering why Lippy Gordon doesn't want to hold my hand—because of my big nose or my wrong-day elephant or my fake warts or something else that I don't know what.

Finally, only because Mr. Sanders told him to and is standing here watching to make sure he does, Hugo Gordon reaches out his hand to me. And then before I know it I'm holding his hand, even folding my fingers over the top.

Hugo's hand is sweaty, just like I knew it would be, but it's more like holding hands with a dog's nose than a sweaty fish. At least that's what I try to think about anyway.

We circle left, all of us. And then we go the other direction, still holding hands. I know it's just circling, but Hugo Gordon, even with his big size, is quick on his feet. Me, I have a little trouble at first going left, but only because my brains are thinking about holding hands with a dog nose and not lefts and rights. Hugo Gordon whispers, "The other way" to me after I step on his foot.

Mr. Sanders says, "Now let's try a do-si-do." And he shows us how. We drop hands, thank lucky stars. Only, my feet do a do-si-don't and I bump right into Hugo's backside. I tell him sorry and then tap my head to get my brains working right. I don't know why my feet are having so much trouble, but it doesn't help that Nancy Jo keeps glaring at me every time I mess up.

Mr. Sanders shows us some other calls like the promenade, allemande, and forward-and-back. I step on Hugo two more times, okay for real four, but I'm hoping nobody is keeping track, including Hugo. I keep looking at the clock on the gym wall, because certainly we've been in here longer than normal and when is the bell going to ring anyway? The clock says there's five minutes left before the end of the period, which I don't see how that can be right. Then Mr. Sanders says, "Should we put this to some music? Sounds like a good idea to me."

That awful music starts up and the calls come fast. *"Bow to your partner, to your corner now too, ladies and gents, listen what you do. Allemande left, ring-a-ding-ding, join hands and circle left till you're back home again. Ladies to the center . . ."*

Somehow I get lost after the bowing part and then I mix up a promenade with an allemande because how are we really supposed to know the difference so fast? And then while everybody else joins hands and goes around left, I get stuck outside the circle going no place.

"What is she doing?" says Nancy Jo as she goes by me.

The song says something about going home again, and that sounds good to me, I'm ready to go home right now. But home must mean something else in square dancing because the song keeps on going and I'm still here.

8.

While I wait for Grandpa Felix to pick me up after school, I take my drawing pad out of my oversize paper bag, the one with my good luck stain on it, along with my No. 2 Hard drawing pencil and start to sketch. I draw whatever I can think of, except I don't draw any squares or dancing shoes. Or hands. Or warts.

If Mister Leonardo da Vinci was here, he would surely say, "Pray tell, if I see another wart ever again it will be too soon I should think."

Grandpa Felix is fifteen minutes late, and when he does pull up in front of the school, he rolls down his window and yells, "We've got to go! Hurry, hurry!"

I stuff my drawing pad under my arm and scramble to his car. As soon as I slide into the passenger seat and shut the door, we're off. "What's the matter?" I ask, and I'm worried that there's been an emergency of some sort. And because sometimes I happen to think about dead things I ask him if it's *that* kind of emergency.

"No, Penelope," he says. "Nobody died." Then he tells me he's sorry he's late, sorry to have to rush me, but he's having a day. "It's madness, what this world has become."

"I know," I say. "They're making us learn square dancing in school."

But he's talking about a different kind of madness and he says he means what's happening at Tom Clarke's photography store. "They're no longer carrying actual film. It's digital everything from now until Sunday and for the rest of our lives."

"Oh," I say. "That's bad." Even though I'm not sure I understand why it *is* so bad. Grandpa has a lot of cameras, and I know he's got some that don't use actual film. (Even though those aren't his all-time favorites.) Alfred does, though. Alfred is the name I gave his 35mm Leica camera, the one he always takes with him to photography jobs, the one that he's had since forever ago.

"The worst was when that young man behind the counter looked at me like I was from the Ice Age," he says. "Like I had just emerged from the tundra wearing clothes from a woolly mammoth's hide. Like I was grunting at him, demanding some ancient form of media that people once called film." Then he grunts, my grandpa Felix does, and I worry that his brains are getting all demented. Which sometimes happens to old people.

I put my hand on his arm as he drives. When we get to a red light, he looks over at me and I say, "Your name is Grandpa Felix. And I am Penelope Crumb, your granddaughter." Because when brains get demented they sometimes need to be reminded of these sorts of things.

He shakes his head. "I know who we are, little darling. It's not us that's the problem."

Then I grunt at him to let him know I understand. He smiles and laughs and grunts back at me. And there we are, just the two of us, driving along and grunting at each other all the way to the newest branch of Portwaller Savings and Loan on Mealey Street.

Grandpa Felix having his own photography business usually means he gets hired to take pictures at weddings or parties, which are really the most fun because there's music and tiny food on white plates, and if you say nice things to the bride about how pretty her dress is, she will usually let you eat some.

But then there are other jobs like ribbon-cutting ceremonies or grand openings of shopping centers that are kind of boring and don't have any food. But sometimes there are extra-large scissors for the cutting of the ribbon, and when nobody is looking I hold them and pretend I own a hair salon for giants. Because giants need a trim every now and then like the rest of us.

Today's job is the grand opening of the newest branch of Portwaller Savings and Loan bank. My job is Photographer's Assistant, which means that I hold Grandpa's cameras and do everything he tells me. It's a very important job even though I only get to take pictures every now and then when Grandpa Felix is in a good mood.

When we pull into the parking lot, Grandpa Felix says, "This probably won't take very long. And don't ask anyone if there's food. Let's just assume there isn't."

I tell him okay and I get out of the car, careful to keep his cameras around my neck from knocking together.

"And don't play with the big scissors," he tells me.

"What?"

He winks. "You didn't know that I knew you did that, did you?"

I say, "I don't know what you're talking about, Grandpa Felix."

There are about six people in the parking lot waiting for us, men and women all dressed up and looking business-y. They all have pretty regular noses, the kind that you'd probably never notice if you weren't looking. But I'm always looking. It's an artist's job to notice these things.

Here's something else I notice: There's nothing much noticeable about any of them. They are all wearing dark blue or gray outfits without any wrinkles or missing buttons and they look fine enough, but just a little too Regular in my opinion. And isn't that a shame. Mister Leonardo da Vinci would say, "Give me a standout feature, something different to lay my eyes upon, and I will paint you a masterpiece."

One of the men, the tallest of them all, looks at his watch and then at Grandpa Felix.

Grandpa says hello and tells them how sorry he is that he is a few minutes late but that he's ready to go. "I was thinking we could start with a shot in front of the new building. There's nice light right now, and you've got a beautiful blue spruce over here." He asks me to hand him Alfred.

When I do, the man with the watch gets a look on his face that says Does That Thing Even Work?

Then he looks at me and says, "Where did you dig that old thing up?"

I'm pretty sure he means the camera and not Grandpa Felix, so I say, "This is Alfred, the same kind of camera that Alfred Einstein used."

"Eisenstaedt," says Grandpa Felix. "She means Alfred Eisenstaedt."

I say, "Right. Him."

The man with the watch says, "We were hoping to see some of the pictures today. I mean, you can do that with a digital camera."

"Yes," says a woman with red painted lips. "We thought you'd be bringing a modern camera so we could see how we look right away."

"You get better quality with these," says Grandpa. "They might be old, but don't judge them by their looks. I can assure you that these cameras are among the best ever made."

The man looks like maybe he isn't so sure, or doesn't have the time to think about how old cameras or photographers are, seeing how he's very busy and important with the money counting and whatever else bankers do, so he just says we should go ahead and get on with it. And not in a very nice way, if you want to know the truth.

The people line up in front of the bank, and Grandpa Felix starts snapping pictures with Alfred and then switches to another camera from around my neck. Grandpa Felix was right about it not taking very long because a little bit later he says, "Well, I think I've got some good ones."

The man with the watch says something that sounds like "I hope so," but I'm not exactly sure, and the others don't say thank you or anything much at all. Grandpa Felix shakes their hands and puts a smile on his face, but I can tell it's not a real smile. Not a true one.

And then we're back in the car on the way home.

"Sometimes I long for the days when I worked with beetles," says Grandpa Felix.

"Beetles?" I say.

"They were quiet and so very easy to get along with," he says. "They didn't care what camera I brought with me. Didn't take one look at this old face and think I'm not up to the job."

"And they probably didn't ask to see the pictures you took, did they?"

"Exactly right," he says. "Not even once."

"And they probably didn't ever call you a name," I say.

"A name?" he says. "No, the thing about beetles is they don't talk, my dear Penelope. But, I'm just being a grump. I'll win these people over, I will. When they see the pictures, when they see, then I'll have them in my corner."

"How?" I say as air from the open car window blows my ponytail forward and tickles my nose.

"Sometimes people can see only one part of other people. Like looking at just a sliver of a photograph or a painting and believing that's all there is. The thing is, my little darling, that's never all there is. There's always more."

"Like the moon," I say.

"What moon?" says Grandpa Felix.

I point out the window where the moon ought to be. "The one up there."

Grandpa looks up through the windshield. "Oh,

that moon. Right. I'm with you." He winks at me and smiles. "What about it?"

"I learned at school that we only ever get to see one side of the moon," I tell him. "I wonder what's on the other side."

"That is something to wonder about."

"I mean, for all we know, the other side could be made out of cotton candy or fizzy water," I say.

"With a bunch of fish people who swim with their elbows," he says.

I laugh. "Who breathe the fizz and have fur instead of scales."

"Fur?" he says.

"Because it's so cold up there, Grandpa Felix."

"Of course," he says. "Makes perfect sense."

I keep my eyes on the moon as Grandpa drives. It follows us, the moon does, and I wonder how we will ever know what really is on the other side. When I ask Grandpa, he says, "From down here, I guess we never will know unless the moon decides to show us. Until then, we can go on just thinking whatever we want."

I nod, but that doesn't seem fair.

"But don't worry," he says, patting my shoulder. "Those bank people will change their tune when they see my pictures. I'll show them that I've got fish that can swim with their elbows, and all will be well."

Then I start to wonder what I could show Nancy Jo and the others to make things all right for me. If they saw my other side of the moon, maybe they would see that I'm no Wartgirl, really. Maybe I could show them the whole me. But how?

When Grandpa pulls up to the front of our apartment, he says, "Can you keep a secret?"

I tell him I can, even though I'm not so sure.

He whispers, "Sometimes, when I've got a problem, I like to sing to the moon."

"Really?"

"Yes, little darling," he says. "That moon is a wonder. And when you sing to it, you let it know. And who knows, maybe if you sing loud enough, the moon might even hear you."

9.

I stare at the moon for most of the night. It stares back, real quiet. Like it's full of secrets it doesn't want to tell. While I'm staring, I take out my drawing pad and No. 2 Hard pencil, open my bedroom window, and stick my head outside for a better look. I reach up at the moon, put my fingers on either side of it, and try to make it turn. But it keeps its distance, that moon does, so I slip back inside.

A couple of times when I'm drawing, the moon slips behind a cloud like maybe it doesn't even want me to see *this* side of it. While it hides, I wonder what the moon can see of me from up there: my room, the messy Heap of clothes in the center of the floor, the drawings on my wall, my big nose. I pull back my curtains so the moon has a clear view.

And when I do, I get the idea that maybe, just maybe, the way to show Nancy Jo and everybody the whole me is to tell them what they don't know about me, what they can't see. On the back of my moon drawing, I start to make a list.

The Other Side of Penelope Crumb

1. I like orange candy, orange Popsicles, and orange soda better than other flavors, but not because of the way they taste. Because orange is the only flavor that is also a color and that is also a fruit, and you've got to appreciate something that's so many different things at once.

2. The only reason I talk about dead things a lot is because I have a Graveyard Dead dad. If I had a dad made out of marshmallows, I'd talk a lot about s'mores, I bet.

3. My brother is an alien. On most days I wish

NASA would take him back to his home planet, but on some days I don't so much.

4. I want to be a famous artist when I grow up, just like Mister Leonardo da Vinci, only not dead.

5. Sometimes, I . . .

Before I can finish number five, my mom peeks into my room and tells me to go to sleep. I tell her I will and then ask, "Tell me something about you that I don't know."

"Tell you something you don't know?" she says.

I nod. "About you."

"How about, I'm very tired and would like to go to bed," she says.

I give her a look that says I'm Serious and then another one right after that says And Make It a Good One.

She bites her lip and I watch her as she thinks of something. "Let's see, let's see. Something you don't know. Hmmm." Finally, she says, "I can't ride a bike. I don't know how."

"For real?" I say.

"We lived in town, growing up. And none of us

had bikes. Your father made me try to ride one, once, after we got married, but I crashed and skinned up my knee before I even made it a few feet." She shrugs. "I haven't been on one since. How's that for something?"

"That's a good one," I say. "And don't worry, I won't tell anyone so you won't feel bad that you can't do something that lots of other people can do, even little kids."

She says, "Penelope Rae." (Jaundiced liver.) And then she turns off my light.

At school the next day, I've got my list in my pocket. I keep it there until gym, and wait on the bleachers for Nancy Jo and the others in my square to arrive. I catch Patsy Cline looking at my hands once, even though she says she isn't at all, but when I show her that the warts have not returned, she smiles and things start to feel almost normal again.

Angus Meeker says he's been practicing and he just knows that he's going to Adventureland, like it's an absolute fact and no one can tell him any different. Vera Bogg, all in pink, says she doesn't like roller coasters anyway, but do you think Adventure-land has a carousel?

Patsy Cline tells them, "Before you all start making any plans, you've first got to win the hoedown, you know."

"Yeah," I say. And then I spot Nancy Jo and Helena and the other fifth graders from my square, everybody except for Hugo. They are starting to climb the bleachers when I pull the list from my pocket and unfold it. Then I get up from my seat and move toward them. But before I can start reading from my list, Nancy Jo sees me and says, "Penelope Crumb, we need to talk." Which is enough of a surprise that I forget about my other side of the moon for a moment. "And get Vera, too."

I wave at Vera to come over to where the rest of our square, minus Hugo, is sitting. "Okay, look," says Nancy Jo. "I really want to win this hoedown. I mean, I think everybody does, but I really, really want to win." And she makes a big deal out of the last *really*. "So we need to be the best. Got it?"

She's looking at me when she says this last part. I nod, happy that she hasn't yet called me Wartgirl, and say, "Where's Hugo?"

Nancy Jo shrugs like it doesn't matter where he is or isn't. But then I see him shuffling into the gym, and he's watching his feet the whole way. "There he is," I say. And I mean it in the way you find a missing sock: happy to have everyone back together in the drawer. But Nancy Jo must think I mean it in a different way, because she laughs, pokes me in the arm for some reason, and says, "Yeah, there he is all right."

Mr. Sanders tells us to get going to our squares and that he has some new calls for us to learn. Then he says he's posted the hoedown rules and scoring system on the wall. And also that he's confirmed that tickets to Adventureland are for each person in the winning square plus an accompanying adult or parent, so stop asking him about it. We should all be focusing on the dancing and not the prize so much, he says. "Now, ladies and gents, squares unite!"

On the way to our square I say hello to Hugo, who is shuffling alongside me.

He grunts something at me that I think might be hi but I'm not really sure. So I say, "Before you got here, Nancy Jo was saying how she really wants to win the hoedown. And that we should all try hard to win or something like that."

Hugo says, "Humph," and then nothing else. Except this: "As long as we're trying, how about you trying not to step on my foot?"

That's what he says. He really does.

Mr. Sanders says, "Let's pick up where we were last time." The music starts, and before I know it I am holding hands with Hugo and am circling right. I manage to circle without stepping on anybody's body parts, thank lucky stars. But watching where my feet are going and listening to the calls in the music at the same time is really hard, if you want to know the truth. Something I am only able to do in short bursts, I guess, because the next calls are strung close together—allemande left, right hand turn, right and left grand, and weave the ring—and once again I am stuck outside the square and really lost.

Hugo tries to pull me back in, but that only makes things worse. Because then when I'm supposed to be weaving and then making a star, I don't know where to go, and that makes Vera Bogg and her partner not know where to go, and pretty soon nobody is going anywhere.

Nancy Jo has her arms crossed and she's giving me a look that says What Is Wrong with You, I Mean Really?

The song goes on for a while longer, a long while, actually, and here we are, our whole square, just standing around in a clump. Everybody's looking at me like this is all my fault, which I know is true, but still.

When the music stops, Mr. Sanders comes over to us and says, "If you make a mistake and the square breaks down, just get back to your home spot in your square and start again with the next call. Everyone makes mistakes, people," he says real loud. "Just try to keep up and do the best you can."

Nancy Jo says to her partner, loud enough that I can hear, "Wartgirl and Lippy are going to make us lose."

My ears start to sweat when I hear that I am Wartgirl again. And I start to get that feeling that I might go dead, but I stop myself somehow, because if I did go dead right here in gym, that would only give them something else to stare and point at.

I want to reach into my pocket and tell them all that there's more to see of me than what they've seen already, there is, I promise. But Wartgirl is in my head now and even if I did pull out my list, I'm pretty sure that to them, right now, my other side of the moon would look just like this side anyway.

10.

After the last bell, I wait in front of the school for Hugo Gordon.

I don't know if Hugo rides a bus or is a walker or gets picked up. But while I wait for him I get out my drawing pad and draw the brick wall that lines the walkway. It's got the name of our school on it: Portwaller Elementary, and there are some cracks in it that if you kind of squint a little look like a frog wearing a crash helmet.

Just when I finish the frog's mouth, I see him. Hugo's not so fast of a walker, so I have time to put my drawing pad and pencil in my bag and catch up with him before he gets to the sidewalk. I holler his name. Not his nickname, his real one.

But he keeps on walking even though I'm right behind him and am pretty sure he can hear me. I call his name again, louder this time, but he doesn't stop until I am right in front of him blocking his way. "Hugo Gordon," I say.

He just stares at me, that boy does, like maybe he doesn't know who I am.

So I tell him. "It's me. Penelope Crumb. Your square-dancing partner. From gym."

He says, "Yes." And he says it like he thinks I was asking him if my name is Penelope Crumb and if I am his dance partner. Which I already know that I am. Both things.

I say, "So I was thinking that if we want to win the hoedown, we could practice. You know, together."

He wipes his lip with the back of his hand.

"What do you think?" I say.

"About what?"

"Good gravy, about practicing," I say.

He shrugs at me and says, "Not interested." Then he starts walking.

I step out of the way and trail after him asking why, why, why, but this Hugo Gordon is really good at pretending I'm not here.

"Don't you want to win?" I ask, not understanding why anyone wouldn't.

"Nope," he says.

"Wait, don't you want to show them?"

He stops and turns around then. "Show them what exactly?"

"You," I say.

"How much more do they need to see?" He holds his arms out to his sides. "I'm pretty sure this is everything."

I'm not sure what to say to that, and he doesn't wait for me to think of something before he goes on down the street. He turns back once, though, just for a second or two, making me wonder.

I knock on Grandpa's door and tell him it's me and to open up. Which is what you have to do if you want him to answer, because otherwise he will think it's somebody asking for money or selling cookies and he'll pretend he's not home.

When he opens the door, he smiles at me and says, "Penelope, little darling, you've made my afternoon."

His small apartment is a mess like regular, but I've seen it in worse shape. He tells me not to mind the mess, and I don't. I walk right over to the kitchen table, sit down, and start to go through the photographs that are in a big heap.

"These are all beetles," I say, holding a close-up of a bright green one with black spots, eight of them, who's climbing on the end of a broken flower stem. He might've been the one that did the breaking, it's hard to tell, but either way he looks like he's holding on for dear life.

"That they are," says Grandpa Felix. "We were talking about them the other day, you know, so I dug some pictures out of my files. Amazing little creepers, aren't they?"

I tell him that they are and then ask about the ones from the bank.

"There were beetles at the bank?" he says with a wink.

I laugh and ask, "Have you gotten them back yet?" Grandpa Felix sends out his film to be developed, and it usually takes a few days to get back the pictures.

"Now that Tom Clarke is no longer dealing in film, I had to send it out to a new place, and as it turns out, they are faster." He picks up a yellow envelope from his coffee table and flicks it with his finger. "Just arrived this morning. Want to see?"

I tell him that I do, and he pulls out a stack of photographs from the envelope and puts them down on the table in front of me. I look over them, slowly and carefully because 1) Grandpa's pictures are like art; and 2) he always asks me what I notice about them and doesn't mean about their noses or their outfits. "The light in this one makes the tops of their heads glow," I say after a time. "Like they're angels or something."

Grandpa nods. "You're right, you're right. Probably not appropriate for bankers."

I look at the rest. "I don't know how you did it, Grandpa, but you've made those people look a lot friendlier in these pictures than they did in real life."

He pinches my cheek and then puts the photographs back into the envelope. "Ah, but will these be enough to do the trick?"

"Definitely," I say. "You'll show them."

"We'll see," he says.

"No, Grandpa," I tell him, "*they* will."

On the way home, Grandpa stops at Marauder's Treat Shop on Thirteenth Street and buys me an orange sherbet shake. While he's trying to decide between a scoop of chocolate marshmallow and rum raisin for himself, I see Tildy, the reason-Terrible-hardly-ever-comes-out-of-his-room Tildy, over by the fudge counter. She's with another girl who's scraping the last bit of something from the bottom of her paper cup. Hot fudge, I'm guessing, because she's got some on the corner of her mouth.

I make my way toward them, pretending to count the flavors in the tubs through the glass display case, and when I get closer, I hear Tildy say, "He didn't talk much. I was the one doing all the talking all the time, you know what I mean? I like to talk, you know, but sometimes you need somebody else to say something once in a while." She pushes up the sleeves of her sweater.

"Exactly right," says the other girl.

"And there's his hair," says Tildy. "I wish it was wavier. You know how much I like wavy hair."

The girl sucks on her spoon. "Wavy hair is the best."

Tildy tells the boy behind the counter that she would like two pieces of peanut butter fudge. Then she turns back to her friend and tells her that she's got some chocolate on her face. The girl wipes at her face with her fingers and Tildy continues. "So, I told him the other day that it's not working. Plus, I think I might've been allergic to his cologne. I was sneezing a lot when I was around him, so that's a biological reason for a breakup right there. And you can't question biology."

"Exactly right," says the other girl again. "Biology rules."

The boy behind the counter hands Tildy her fudge, and she pays. I'm right behind Tildy now, and for some reason, hearing them talk about Terrible like this makes my ears burn. So I say, "There's a lot more to him than you can see." But I'm actually not sure this is true seeing how he's an alien and all, so I add, "Probably."

Tildy almost drops her fudge. She turns around and when she sees me, her face gets Wild Strawberry Red. "Oh, Penelope," she says. "I didn't see you there."

I tell her that it sounds like she has a lot of trouble seeing people lately. And that's when Grandpa Felix comes over to me with his scoop of rum raisin and tells me it's time to go. Then he says hello to Tildy and takes my elbow.

Once we're in the car again, I say, "You know who that was, don't you?"

"I do," says Grandpa.

"Did you hear what she was saying?"

"I try not to listen in on other people's conversations." And he gives me a look that says And I

Would Advise You to Do the Same. He clears his throat. "But this one, I happened to hear without trying."

We pull up to the front of our building and I thank Grandpa for the shake. Just as I'm about to open the door, Grandpa points out the car window and says, "Isn't that Terrence?"

I look where he's pointing. It *is* Terrible. He's sitting on the front step of our building staring at his shoestrings.

"Oh dear," says Grandpa. "Maybe we should drive around the block a couple of times before you go in, you know, to give him some space."

I reach for the door handle and say, "Grandpa Felix, I don't think there's enough space in the universe."

I wonder, as I walk toward him, if there's ever more than one side to an alien. The closer I get, though, watching him sit there, with his head resting in his hands, he looks more like my brother than Terrible, truth be told, he does, and I decide that there must be.

I sit down beside him and stare into the street, just like he's doing. He doesn't call me Dufus or knuckle-punch me in my shoulder, and after a long time of just sitting and staring, I hand him my orange sherbet shake. And without saying a word, he drinks the whole thing.

11.

School starts out regular the next day. Miss Stunkel goes over what she's going to make us learn this morning: decimals, decimals, and other boring math things, I'm pretty sure.

But then things get a little un-regular when Miss Stunkel says the afternoon periods are being canceled because there's an assembly about fire safety in the gymnasium that has been rescheduled from last month.

Normally I would be happy about this because 1) no afternoon periods means no gym, and 2) no gym means no square dancing. But now that I'm trying to get Hugo Gordon to practice with me so that we can win the hoedown so that everybody can see what they don't already and will stop calling me Wartgirl, a fire safety assembly is the kind of thing that's called In the Way.

All morning long, Angus Meeker goes on about his uncle who is a firefighter and how he's the greatest because he drives a pickup truck and makes his own beef jerky. "He's going to be here, I bet," he says. "He'll probably give us a special tour of the fire truck, if I ask him."

Patsy Cline says, "They won't make the sirens go, will they?"

"Probably," says Angus.

"Maybe you could ask him not to?" says Patsy Cline.

"Why would I do a dumb thing like that for?" he says.

Vera Bogg says, "Yeah, why?"

Patsy Cline says, "Never mind, forget all about it, why don't you."

But since Patsy Cline and me used to be best friends, I know certain things about her. For example, I know that Patsy Cline's ears are real sensitive to loud noises, on account of the fact that they are giant-size. Not very many people know this, though, because she keeps them covered up real good with her thick, frizzed-out hair.

So I say, "Not everybody enjoys sirens," without mentioning anything about Patsy Cline's ears, because if Patsy Cline doesn't want Vera and Angus to know how big they are, then I guess I'm not going to be the one to tell them.

Patsy Cline smiles at me. Angus gives me a look that says Are You Crazy, Sirens Are the Best Part. And Vera looks from Patsy Cline to me like she doesn't know what she's missed.

On the way to the fire safety assembly, Angus says, "You know the Monster Truck Monster Showdown that's coming here next month? My uncle, the one that's a firefighter, he's going to take me. He is. He's going to take me."

"I don't see what's so fun about monster trucks," says Vera Bogg. "They're just trucks with big wheels, aren't they?"

"Tires," says Angus. "They're called tires." He pushes past me, Vera, and Patsy Cline and pulls open the door to the gym.

"Whoa," I say. There is a house in the gym. Or half a house, actually, one that's been sliced right down the middle so you can see into each room. And there are firefighters in their yellow suits handing out pamphlets. One of them even has on one of those masks that makes him look like Darth Vader if Darth Vader ever came to Portwaller Elementary wearing yellow fire pants with suspenders.

Angus runs off to find his uncle. And Vera Bogg, who is wearing a pink-and-pink-striped outfit, says she hopes that we don't have to crawl around on the floor and do stop, drop, and roll like we did last year, because this is a new dress.

"When there's a fire, you can't worry about getting your clothes all dirtied up," I tell her.

"This isn't a real fire, Penelope Crumb." And then she says to Patsy Cline, "You don't think there will be a real fire in here, do you?"

Patsy Cline tells her no, and that she's pretty sure

they would need our parents' permission to have a real fire at school. And that she doesn't remember there being a permission slip sent home for her mom to sign. Patsy Cline is very good about remembering those kinds of things.

Vice Principal Hardy has a microphone and he introduces a firefighter captain who tells us a lot about fire safety, things like using fireplace screens, not jamming an outlet full of plugs, not playing with matches. Then he says that they've set up this pretend house here so that we can walk through it in small groups and point out things that are both wrong and dangerous.

The lower grades go through the house first while we fourth graders and fifth graders wander around to the different tables and push the buttons on smoke detectors and try on firefighter hats. Patsy Cline covers her ears and stays away from the smoke detectors for the most part.

I follow her over to the station where the firefighters are letting people try on their outfits, and while Patsy Cline looks for a hat that covers her ears, I see

Hugo. He's got on a firefighter's hat and a yellow coat that is too long but barely fits across the middle. And he's just there, standing by himself, and if he wasn't so big, he'd probably be invisible.

I get right beside him and wait for him to look over at me. It doesn't happen. I clear my throat at him. Twice.

"What?" he says after a while. "Are you going to say that more people die from corn or something than in fires?"

"Corn?" I say, watching the sweat build on his lip. "No, I wasn't going to say that." And then I start to wonder how you could go dead from corn, if that's possible.

"Good."

"I can't eat corn," I say. "It gives me an upset stomach."

Hugo Gordon looks like he wants to say something, but he just wipes his lip, which is just in time because those beads of sweat looked like they were about to spill into his mouth.

"So about practicing," I say.

"Why do you keep bothering me?"

"This isn't called bothering you," I tell him. "This is called helping."

"I don't need help." He wipes his lip again.

"Yes you do," I say. Because for one thing, there's Lippy, but I don't say anything about that. When you want to help someone it's best not to remind him of the awful name people call him.

"No I don't," he says.

"Yes you do. You just don't know it."

Hugo looks at me then and says, "Maybe you're the one who needs help. I know what they call you."

"Well, duh," I say. "Of course I need help. Why do you think I'm here? If you could help me be a better square dancer, maybe we could win the hoedown and then they could stop calling me that name."

"Why should I help you?" he says.

Good gravy. That's not a question I was expecting to hear because helping me means helping him, too. No more Wartgirl, but no more Lippy Gordon, either. I tell him that he'd win, too. No more sitting by himself at the cafeteria or in the bleachers. "Don't you know what they call *you*?" I ask.

"I know," he says. "And I know that you pretended to have warts on your hands so you wouldn't have to hold hands with me. I may be fat, but I am not slow, Penelope Crumb."

My word. I don't know what to say to that, but even if I did, there's no time, because Vice Principal Hardy gets on his microphone and says that the fourth and fifth graders can now tour the house. Hugo hands his coat and hat back to one of the firefighters. I follow him into the house.

"Would you leave me alone, please?" he says kind of loud. And his words have rocks in them. People start to look at us, and because if there's one thing we don't need it's more attention, I leave him alone and instead go into the kitchen where there's all kinds of dangerous things happening on the stove. I point each one out to the firefighter nearby and he nods and says I can climb out the window if I want.

I give him a look that says For Real?

"To practice your fire escape," he explains. Then he shows me some carpeted steps that lead to the window.

I tell him okay, and he holds on to my elbow as I climb the stairs and swing my legs out the window. Once my feet hit the ground, I can see other people following behind me, including Nancy Jo. But she's having some trouble with her exit. Her foot gets caught in the frame and while she tries to free it, she tumbles out of the window and lands on her knees.

She hollers, that Nancy Jo does, but gets quickly to her feet. And then she does something I don't really understand: She looks at the knees of her pants, I mean, really looks at them. For what, I'm not sure, until I hear her ask another fifth-grade girl nearby to see if there are any rips.

"I don't see any," says the girl.

"Are you sure?" says Nancy Jo. And she almost looks like she is going to cry. "Look really close. Are you sure there aren't any?"

The girl says she's pretty sure, and that's when I decide to go over. "Do you need some help?" I say.

Nancy Jo gives me a look that says What Do You Want?

I say, "I think your pants look fine. You can't tell you fell out a window or anything."

And then she turns to the fifth-grade girl and says, "Can you check one more time?" The girl asks her to spin around and when she does, she says, "Nancy Jo, they are fine, I promise."

Nancy Jo looks relieved, she really does. I don't know why she would get so worked up about messing up her pants in the first place, but I figure now might be a good time to show her some things about me. I pull out my Other Side list from my pocket and say, "One time, when I was little, a window shut on my hand and my fingernail turned black and then fell off."

I tell her this because 1) it has to do with windows; and 2) it might make her feel better to know that a lot worse can happen to you than a rip in your pants.

It works, too. Nancy Jo must start feeling much more like her regular awful self because then she makes a comment about the warts that I do not have and no longer want even if I could get them, but I can't hear all of what she says because right then, I see Hugo Gordon in the window. And he's stuck.

The firefighter is trying to pull him back inside the house, but Hugo's foot is caught about the same place Nancy Jo's was, and Hugo doesn't have the kind of body that's called limber. Meanwhile another firefighter shows up to try to pull him from the outside. Hugo's face is going red, and I'm not sure if it's because he's stuck halfway in and out of a window or because lots of kids are starting to gather around to see which firefighter is going to win Hugo Tug-of-War.

Awful Nancy Jo points at him and says something about getting some margarine to grease him up like a turkey. But it's not funny, and I tell her so. Then I say, "Not everybody can be as good at climbing out of windows as you, Nancy Jo." You know, because she *isn't*.

That gets her quiet for a minute. Long enough for the firefighters to get Hugo's leg free and push him out the window. He lands on his feet, thank lucky

stars, but just barely, and then he wipes his lip with his shirtsleeve. He only looks up at the crowd of kids around him for a second or two, and when he does he's got a look on his face that I take to mean There Is No Winning for Lippy Gordon.

So I give him one back that says There Can Be, If We Try.

12.

Littie Maple is at my door with her hands full. I tell her to come on in and then I say, "Did you find some?"

She spreads out the papers on our coffee table. "Of course. You can find anything on the Internet. Even instructions on square dancing. I also found a list of calls," she says. "Calls are the dance steps that you're supposed to do."

I tell her I know what calls are, thanks.

"Now, I figure I'll be the Caller," says Littie. "We just need to get you a partner."

I look at the clock on the wall. "He's supposed to

be here by now." I gave Hugo Gordon my address after the Window Incident and he didn't actually say he would come, but he didn't say he wouldn't, either.

"Until he does, how about I do some calling and you do some dancing," says Littie. "Stand in your square."

I tell her okay and then face the front door.

Littie reads from one of the printouts: "It says, 'Bow to your partner.'" She looks at me and the empty space beside me and says, "Well, we can probably just skip that part." She goes on. "Heads forward and back."

"Am I a head?" I say.

"I don't know," says Littie. "Are you?"

"Mr. Sanders didn't say anything about being a head."

Littie says, "Do you want to be a head?"

I shrug.

Littie says, "You could be a side. If you're not a head. Apparently you can be a head or a side. If I were you, I would be a head. I'm just saying."

"Do you have to do more dancing when you're a head? Because maybe a side would be better for me."

Littie looks at the paper. "It doesn't say anywhere here that the heads have to do more dancing."

"I bet they do. Because you know how when you go to a restaurant and there is the main meal and then the sides?" I say. "You know, like mashed potatoes or applesauce. Sides."

Littie says, "I know what sides are, Penelope."

"Macaroni can be a side, too. But it can also be the main meal that you order. It can be both," I say. "Except for macaroni, sides aren't as important as the other food on the menu. They just aren't."

"And is that a good thing?" asks Littie.

"Only if they don't have to dance as much."

Littie Maple gives me a look that says I'm Lost.

So I tell her, "Okay, I've decided. I'll be a head as long as I can be macaroni."

She shakes her head at me I don't know what for. "Okay, macaroni, go forward and back."

I step into the center of the square with one big step and then go back.

Littie tells me that's fine and then says, "Now do-si-do."

I do. Sort of. And I have to say it's a lot easier to do when there's nobody to do-si-do around. But Littie says, "I don't think that's right. But it's hard to say for sure without a partner." Then she says, "Is your brother home?"

I tell her to forget about it. But she won't. Instead she says, "Do you want to win or not?"

I start to say yes, I do, but . . . but I don't have a chance to say anything because there goes Littie Maple down our hallway toward Terrible's room. Worse than that, she comes back with him.

"What are you doing now, Dorkus?" he says to me.

"She needs you to be her square-dancing partner," says Littie.

"Littie Maple!" I say. "You're supposed to be helping. And this is not helping."

"She can forget it," Terrible says. Like I'm not standing right here.

"No," I say, "*he* can. Forget it, I mean." Then I

give Littie a look that says What's the Matter with Your Brains?

Littie Maple rolls her eyeballs and tells Terrible that he doesn't have to dance or anything but just stand there like a statue. Just so that I have something to dance around. And just until my partner shows up, if he's ever going to.

Terrible: "No way."

Me: "Can't we just put a pillow on the floor?"

Littie: "I think a real person would be better since your partner is a real person and not a pillow. I'm just saying."

Me: "What about two pillows?"

Terrible: "I'm out of here."

Littie: "No, wait! Penelope is really bad at this."

Me: "You're a true friend, Littie Maple."

Terrible: "So you're saying you just want me to stand here and watch her act like a big idiot?"

Littie: "That's what I'm saying."

Terrible: "Where do you want me to stand?"

Littie goes through the calls one by one, and you'd think she's been square-dancing since forever or been square-dancing at least once, the way she's acting. She tells me what I'm doing wrong, wrong, wrong. Which apparently is a lot. And then Terrible starts in on me.

"You are just supposed to stand there," I tell him. "And since when do you know anything about square dancing, anyway?"

"I know enough to know that you're not any good," he says.

Well then.

Littie says, "Maybe we should take a break."

I tell her fine and then I go out our door stomping my feet because sometimes there's not enough air in our tiny apartment. I head toward the stairs and decide to find better air outside, the kind of air that doesn't make you feel bad about not being very good at dancing.

But before I can find any of that kind of air, there sitting at the top of the stairs, looking extra sweaty, is Hugo Gordon.

13.

Y ou came," I say. "What are you doing sitting out here?"

"Did you know your building doesn't have an elevator?" he says, wiping his lip.

"Yeah, but it's only three stories. It's a walk-up. You get used to it after a while." He's breathing kind of hard and his face is really red. "Are you okay?" I say.

"But, I mean, what if you had something really heavy to carry?" he says. "You know, like a TV or something."

I shrug. "My brother usually helps my mom with

the heavy stuff. If he's not in a mood or in his room moping. Aliens are really strong."

"Aliens?" says Hugo.

"Don't worry," I say, "he's not the face-eating kind."

"That's a lot of steps," he says.

"So," I say, not sure why Hugo is still sitting on the top of the stairs and going on about not having an elevator when we have a hoedown to practice for. "So, I was just practicing in there." I point down the hall at the door to our apartment.

Hugo wipes his forehead on his shirtsleeve. "Could I maybe have a drink of water?"

I ask him again if he's okay, and he says, "Fine, just fine." So I tell him sure he can have all the water he wants and then I watch as he gets to his feet. He follows me to our apartment door and when I open it, Littie is right there. "Where did you run off to?" she says.

"Nowhere," I say. And then I step out of the way so that Hugo Gordon can come inside. I introduce him to Littie and then go get his water. He drinks the whole thing at once and hands me back the empty cup. I guess when your lip sweats as much as his does, you need to drink a lot.

"Where's Terrible?" I say.

Littie says, "He said he was tired of waiting and . . ."

"And what?"

"And other things that weren't very nice about your dancing," she says.

Oh.

Hugo wipes his lip and says, "Okay, what do you want me to do?"

I point to where the square is and we stand side by side and hold hands just like we did in gym. Littie starts the calling. We bow to each other, Hugo and me, and that part goes fine, even the hand-holding. Hugo's got a serious look on his face, I notice, real serious, and I have a hard time figuring out whether he's being serious about dancing because he wants to win or something else.

Littie continues with the calls and I'm doing an okay job. At least, I've hardly stepped on Hugo's feet. But I must not be doing as good as I think, because Hugo stops dancing at one point, just stops right in the middle of a promenade or lemonade or some other kind of −ade, I'm not sure which, and says, "What are you doing?"

"Square dancing?" I say.

He shakes his head at me and drops my hand.

Littie shows me the instructions she's printed out from the Internet and says I'm doing it wrong. "You need to be over here when you go around," she tells me, pointing to the other side of Hugo. Then she comes over to where Hugo and I are standing and grabs his hands. "Like this."

Hugo says to me, "Maybe you should be the Caller for a little while so you can see how Littie and I do the steps. Maybe that would help."

I don't like this idea at all. But I take the paper from Littie and start yelling out calls. Littie swings and circles and do-si-dos and promenades without stepping on Hugo Gordon at all, as far as I can tell, and they're both smiling about it.

"Are you sure you never square-danced before?" I ask Littie.

She says she's sure and then she says this: "It's not really that hard, Penelope."

My cheeks burn at that, and I say, "Well, that's because I was doing the calling a lot slower than you were, Littie Maple. Try it again."

Littie and Hugo get back to their places in the square, and Littie gives me a sideways look that says What Are You Up To?

I fill my lungs with air and then start calling. Real fast. I start with the bow nice and easy and then spring into the calls one after the next. They start to run together, those calls do, as fast as I'm yelling them, until there's just a stream of square-dancing words shooting out of my mouth. Hugo and Littie try to keep up at first, but the faster I go, the smaller their square gets and then they are just spinning in place.

Littie Maple stops first and puts her hands on her hips. "Just what do you think you're doing?" she says at me, out of breath. Hugo leans against the wall, and he's going to need another drink of water, I'm pretty sure.

I give her a look that says I Don't Know What You Are Talking About.

"I'm just trying to help," she says.

I tell her that she doesn't have to do so good a job at it, if she wants to know the truth. And also that I don't believe she's never square-danced before, no matter how many times she claims she hasn't.

Hugo Gordon says, "I better be going on home."

"But I hardly got to practice," I say.

"See you tomorrow at school," he says. And then he's out the door before I can say anything.

Littie Maple says, "I'd better be going, too. Momma will be needing my help with supper."

And here I am, left all by myself with just some paper instructions and an invisible square.

14.

At school, Patsy Cline and Vera Bogg are talking about how they can't wait for gym because isn't square dancing a lot more fun than everybody thought it was going to be?

"No," I say. "It definitely is not."

Patsy Cline smiles and says, "Especially the music."

I wonder about Patsy Cline sometimes. But if she doesn't know the music is the worst, then I guess I'm not going to be the one to tell her.

While Mr. Sanders is sifting through a bunch of music trying to decide which songs he wants to make us dance to, Nancy Jo tells us to come close because she has got a plan. She looks over her shoulder to make sure none of the other squares is listening, and then she whispers, "I've been thinking. Since some of us just aren't getting the steps," and she looks right at me, "we need to work really hard on the other parts that will get us points so we can win."

"Like what?" I say.

Nancy Jo says, "I was just getting to that." She looks over her shoulder again. "Like dress attire. Mr. Sanders said that each person scores points for how they are dressed, but the square gets points on that, too. So I think we should all wear similar outfits. Boys in black pants and black shirts, and girls in white dresses."

Vera Bogg says, "I'd rather wear pink. Can't we wear pink?"

Nancy Jo tells Vera no, as a matter of fact, we can't. Vera asks why not, and then Nancy Jo says, "Remember, Vera, we are also being scored on attitude."

"Oh," says Vera.

"What about synchronicity and timing?" says Helena.

"We're judged as a square on that," says Nancy Jo. "But don't count on getting a lot of points for either of those, you know, because of Penelope." Like I'm not even standing right in front of them.

Helena laughs, and I pretend I'm not here. I'm so good at it that Nancy Jo notices almost right away. And she must not like it so much when people pretend not to be interested in the things coming out of her mouth because she presses her lips together so tight they practically disappear. And after that happens she gets louder and louder about whatever it is she's saying, and somehow I get better and better at pretending she's not saying anything. I wonder if this is how Hugo got so good at being alone.

We make it through square dancing, Hugo and me, but I have to say, I'm not getting much better. Truth be told, I might even be getting worse. But Hugo doesn't say anything about me stepping on him, running into him, or going the wrong way. But that could be because he doesn't say anything at all really.

I wait for him by the front of the school near the brick wall and the cracks in the shape of the frog. Only there are cracks that I never noticed before, or maybe they're new ones, but they look like the frog is growing another leg. And five legs on a frog just isn't right. I mean for one thing, what would the other frogs say?

While I'm drawing, a shadow hangs over me and the frog. I look up and there is Angus Meeker. "What does that frog have an extra leg for?" he says.

I shrug. "In case he loses one of the others?"

"Speaking of losing," he says, "I saw what happened in gym."

"So?" I tap my pencil on my drawing pad.

He smiles at me. "I'm just saying that we don't have to worry about you guys winning."

I tell him that there's still oodles of time between now and the hoedown, and he says, "Don't take this wrong, but there aren't enough oodles to get you even to the parking lot of Adventureland. But don't worry, I'll tell you all about the Spin Rocket coaster."

Well.

Angus goes then, thank lucky stars, and soon after, Hugo Gordon walks right on by me and barely stops when I tell him that maybe we need another plan to fix things seeing how unless I get good soon I don't know how we can win.

He says, "There is no we." And he makes a big deal out of the *we*.

But I don't see how he could really mean that, considering WE both have names WE don't want and that both of US have the kind of problem that is called Desperate.

I tell him this as I follow him home. Hugo Gordon lives in an apartment, but it's a bigger building than ours and has ten floors. I know that because when I get into the elevator behind him there are ten buttons to push.

"Where are you going?" he asks me, holding the elevator door open with his foot even though we are both safely inside and ready to go up.

"I told you," I say. "We need a new plan."

He rolls his eyeballs at me and wipes his lip. But he moves his foot out of the way of the elevator doors so they close. And then he pushes the button for the seventh floor.

"Number seven," I say. "That's good luck."

When the elevator doors open on his floor, we get out and he says, "Elevators. See how nice they are?"

"It was only three floors," I say under my breath.

He takes out a key on a long string from his backpack and unlocks the door to his apartment. Even before he opens the door, I can hear yelling. I must take a step backward or something because Hugo looks at me and says, "That's just my older sisters. They're loud."

He's right. They are. And when we get inside, one sister has another sister pinned to the floor in the living room. "Hugo!" the one on top shouts. "How's it going?" Then she yanks the ponytail of the sister on the bottom so her head turns toward us.

"Hey, Hugo," she says, the one on the bottom. "Who's your friend?"

Hugo tells them my name is Penelope and that we are sort of working on a school project together or something but not really. That's what he says: "We're sort of working on a school project together or something but not really." Good gravy. Then he tells me that these are his sisters Marta and Veronica and that there's a third sister named Toni who's probably in her room.

Hugo says, "Where's Mom?"

Veronica and Marta roll around on the floor and it's hard to tell exactly, but they look like they are fighting over a rubber band, and while they pull at each other's hair, one of them, I'm not sure who, says, "Mom is at the market but will probably be home any minute so you better give me back that rubber band before I tell her you took them all and now I don't have anything to pull my hair back with, thanks to you."

The sister with the rubber band makes a comment about the other sister's gross hair and asks if she ever heard of a thing called a hairbrush.

Hugo tells me to follow him, and we go into the

kitchen where it's a little quieter but not really. "Do you want some water?" he asks me.

I tell him okay and then ask if he has any more sisters or any brothers or just the three loud ones.

He says it's just him and his mom and three sisters, but doesn't say anything about his dad. Which makes me wonder if he is Graveyard Dead, too, like mine. I ask him, and he looks at me like I just asked him if those are his real teeth.

"I'm not being rude," I say. "I have a dad who is Graveyard Dead and sometimes I just talk about dead things. It's normal."

He takes a drink of water and after putting his empty glass in the sink, he says, "Not dead. Divorced."

"Oh."

"Yeah," he says, "oh."

He tells me he'll be right back and that he is going to put his backpack in his room. I follow him, because I don't want to be left alone with his sisters, seeing how rubber bands are something they really want to have and I happen to have four of them in my ponytail.

Hugo opens the door to his room and I peer inside. "Whoa," I say, "what is that?"

He jumps a little, like he didn't know I was behind him. "Nothing," he says.

But it's not nothing. It very much is the most unnothing thing I've ever seen. "It's a . . ."

"It's not a dollhouse, if that's what you're thinking," he says. "I don't play with dolls."

"It looks kind of like a dollhouse, but bigger and a lot better," I say. One whole wall of Hugo's room is covered with shoeboxes, turned on their sides and stuck together. Inside each box is a room or a scene with people in it. Some are made out of toothpicks and some out of cotton swabs. With really tiny clothes and felted hair. "You made this?"

He nods. In one shoebox there's a family sitting down at a toothpick table for breakfast. In another, there's a hang glider suspended by string over a cardboard mountain. And in another, a tent that looks like it's made out of painted newspaper next to a tiny sleeping bag under a full Styrofoam moon. There's a toothpick man looking up at it.

"Do you get to see him much?" I say.

"Who?"

"Your dad." Because that's one difference between having a dad who is Graveyard Dead and one who is divorced: You probably get to see him a lot more.

Hugo wipes his lip with his shirtsleeve. "Not really. Some, I guess. He has a new family."

"Oh." And then I look back at the toothpick man and wonder if he could be singing to the moon like Grandpa does. "What do you think is on the other side of that moon?" I ask. "The side that we don't ever get to see."

"The same as what's on this side, I guess," he says. "Only dark."

"But maybe it's different," I tell him. "You don't know. Maybe there's something really special."

"Not likely," he says.

I don't see how that can be true, considering all of these shoeboxes that are right in front of me. "Maybe the other side is all wet," I say, remembering Grandpa Felix's and my idea about fur-covered fish people.

"What's that supposed to mean?" says Hugo. He looks hurt but I can't imagine why, unless he's got something against swimming with elbows, so I tell him it means nothing other than that maybe the other side of the moon could be all wet. And I say the words again REAL SLOW while I watch his face because I don't know which word he doesn't like. But I only get a couple of them out, because he stops me and says, "Are you making fun of me?"

I tell him no way, I'm definitely not.

He sighs. "Sorry, I thought maybe you were because I sometimes, you know, sweat a little."

A little, is what he says. I say, "Oh, you do?" Because if he doesn't know that he sweats very much more than a little, then I'm not going to be the one to tell him.

"I can't help it," he says. "It just happens."

I say, "Sometimes I talk to Leonardo da Vinci." Because when somebody shows you their other side of the moon, it's only right that you show them yours.

"Leonardo da Vinci?" he says.

"He's a dead artist," I say. "A real famous one."

"I know who he is," says Hugo. "Does he talk back?"

"Of course." I turn the Styrofoam moon in the shoebox. "It wouldn't be very much fun if he didn't."

15.

Hugo agrees to practice square dancing with me one night a week after school, which isn't a lot, but it's something. Practicing makes me a little better, just like I knew it would, but when I tell this to Hugo he gives me a look that says You Still Stink. Then he says, "Everybody still calls you Wartgirl, you know."

This is not true, I tell him, not *everybody*. Because really it's just Nancy Jo and a couple of others, and just because they have the biggest mouths at Portwaller Elementary it only *seems* like it's everybody saying that awful thing, when really it's just a couple of people WHO ARE VERY MUCH THE LOUDEST.

Hugo just shakes his head at me and tells me to watch out for his feet.

On the evenings when me and Hugo don't practice, Littie Maple steps in to help. Once in a while Terrible helps, too. He shouts out calls as he walks through the living room on the way to the kitchen or something: "Dorks circle right," for example, is one of his favorites.

Still, even with all of this help, somehow I worry, what if it isn't enough?

Grandpa Felix is as busy as ever with his photography jobs. Which means I am busy, too. And, thank lucky stars, there's a wedding. The nice bride lets me eat some of the tiny food at the reception, and while Grandpa Felix is changing film in his cameras, I load up a plate. For real, three.

The wedding is at a place called Riverside Gardens, which doesn't make much sense to me because, for one thing, there's no river that I can find.

And for another, the garden is more like a couple of rosebushes and a fountain. But still, it's very pretty. Which is what I tell the bride before she tells me to help myself to the food.

I carry the plates back into the Riverside Garden house where Grandpa is, but first I have to weave through the crowd of people heading for the dance floor, go past the band, and up the creaky wooden steps and onto the wide porch.

"There you are," says Grandpa Felix. "I see you made friends with the bride."

I nod. "I brought you some food."

He pops a tiny puffball into his mouth. It's stuffed with I don't know what exactly, but I know it's delicious because I've had four. "Wow," he says.

I say, "I know."

He licks his finger. "The groom asked for some candid shots from up here."

"I like weddings," I say.

"You do?"

"Better than banks."

Grandpa Felix adjusts the light meter and then

holds Alfred up to his eye. "Banks? Well, I guess I'd have to agree with you there."

"Did you win over Portwaller Savings and Loan yet?" I ask.

He adjusts the focus. "Win them over?"

"Did you show them your pictures and did they like them is what I mean," I tell him.

"Oh that." He clears his throat. "They asked for a reshoot."

"Good gravy, what didn't they like about them?"

Grandpa Felix tells me to put down my plates and when I do he takes my hands and starts dancing side to side. The band is singing something about going walking after midnight in the moonlight. Which sounds kind of nice if you live in a safe neighborhood and it isn't raining. "Grandpa," I say, keeping my feet planted, "I'm no good."

"Nonsense," he says.

"For real," I say. "I'm the worst at dancing. Everybody at school thinks so."

He looks around and then up. "Well, there's nobody on the porch at the moment but you and me and the moon." He's still dancing while I just stand here, but he starts to turn and then I have no choice except to move my feet.

"There you are," he says, smiling. "We're dancing."

Truth be told, dancing with Grandpa Felix is a lot easier than square-dancing, because all we do is sway. Real slow. I hardly even have to pick up my feet. And there's no square and there's nobody yelling calls at you and telling you what to do.

We keep on swaying back and forth and after a while I can sway without thinking about it so much, until I'm not thinking about it at all, really. That gives my brains room to think about other things. "So what didn't they like about them?" I ask again.

"Who?"

"The bank people."

"You're still on that?" he says.

I tell him I am.

He looks up again and shakes his head. "Some moon."

"Like someone used all of their yellow paint

on that moon and only had a little left over for the stars," I say.

"It may look yellow tonight, from here, but actually the moon isn't yellow at all," he says. "You know that, right?"

I tell him that I do, and that the solar system is one of the things Miss Stunkel is making us learn about.

Then he starts singing something about flying to the moon and swinging on the stars to see what it could be like on Jupiter or Mars. I don't know the words, so I just hum along and watch as the moon slips behind a cloud. We're so small, looking up at it, so small, Grandpa and me, we might as well be in one of Hugo's shoeboxes.

"What if you try, I mean really try, and take a whole bunch of new pictures and they don't like any of them?" I say. "What then?"

He shrugs and musses my hair. "Don't worry so much. Besides, it's my problem, not yours."

But it *is* my problem. Because what happens when people see your other side and it's still not good enough, when it doesn't make any difference?

Then Grandpa Felix says, "I'm going to try something fancy now." And he lets go of one of my hands and takes the other one over my head like he wants to spin me. But I don't figure that out right away so I get all wobbly in the feet and then he takes a step forward and lands his foot on top of mine.

I wince. He says he's sorry and am I all right?

I wiggle my foot and then smile. "I think you might've killed it."

"It'll live," he says. "That's what I get for trying out a fancy move. I should just stick with taking pictures."

"I must get my bad dancing from you. That and my big nose. Thanks a lot, Grandpa."

"You're welcome, little darling," he says. "Now how about another one of those puffballs?"

16.

On Sunday night, I call Patsy Cline to make sure tomorrow is the for real Be an Animal Day so I won't be the only elephant at the zoo. She says it is, she's one hundred percent sure and that she *was* going to be a cow, which is her favorite animal of all time, except that cows have tails. So instead she says she is going to be a clam.

Even though Patsy Cline swears on her singing voice that this Monday is the right Monday, I'm still a little nervous about wearing my costume and won't be okay about being an elephant until I see another animal arrive at Portwaller Elementary and know for certain that I haven't got my days mixed up again. I hide in the bushes out front until the first bus pulls up. Thank lucky stars, to my relief there are some dogs and cats and one unicorn that get off. And a bunch of things that I guess are supposed to be animals but look more like kids with cotton ball tails over their jeans and who look like they didn't really want to be animals in the first place. Or else they are just really bad at being anything other than themselves.

Then, I see an enormous fish slowly making its way down the sidewalk. It's got shiny metallic scales, this fish does, all different colors that when they catch the light they glisten and almost look like they are moving. There are fins and a fishtail and a giant mouth that drapes over the kid's head like a hood.

I poke my head out of the bushes so I can get a better look, and that's when I catch a glimpse of the kid's face and his shiny lip. I jump out of the bushes and yell, "Hugo!"

He must not recognize me in my elephant costume because he gives out a sort of high-pitched wail and drops his backpack.

I pull off my elephant nose and say, "It's me. Penelope Crumb."

"I know who it is," he says, slowly bending over and reaching for his backpack. I pick it up for him and put it back in his fin. "Why did you have to leap out at me like that?" he says.

I tell him because I'm an elephant, why else? And he says that makes no sense because elephants don't leap, they trudge. And don't I know anything?

"You don't have to be mean," is what I tell him. Then I say, "Did you make that costume all by yourself?"

"Yeah, so?"

"So?" I say. "It's the best costume of a fish that I've ever seen." Not that I've seen a lot of fish costumes, but I've seen a lot of fish and Hugo Gordon looks just like one. "How long did it take you?"

He says a couple of weeks because of all the scales.

"You're really good at making things," I say.

He smiles a little, and when he does, I see his

lip is so full of sweat and he's not wiping it off. The beads just keep coming and coming and I guess because he's a fish he probably can't get his fin up to his mouth to take care of it. He wiggles his nose and tries to get his tongue up there to lick it away, which is kind of gross, but what else can he do?

I must be staring at the whole thing for a while because then Hugo looks right at me and says, "What are you looking at?"

"Your lip," I say, because for one thing, he asked. And for another, he should really have thought about what to do about that because this is a real problem and people are going to notice.

He turns red in the face. Then he swings his backpack at me. I step out of the way in time, thank lucky stars. Elephants have good reflexes.

"Sorry," he says. "The front pocket."

"What?"

"Can you um, unzip the pocket?" he says. His lip is really soaked now, something like I've never seen. I don't know where it all comes from, and I don't know how much more there is to come out. So

I quick unzip the front pocket of his backpack before we're both washed away by the flood and I find a pack of tissues stuffed inside. "Here," I say, handing him the whole pack. Because, truth be told, he's going to need more than one.

He fumbles with the pack awhile and then it falls to the sidewalk. I pick it up and hand it to him again. This happens two more times—he fumbles it, drops it, and I pick it up. And the last time, when I pick it up he tells me he's going to need my help.

Right away I think he wants me to mop his lip with a tissue. I give him a look that says I Do Not Want to Do That. And then I say, "I do not want to do that." Just in case he's not very good at telling what different kinds of faces mean and also because I really mean it.

But he says, "Just put a couple of them in my fin."

Okay then.

I pull a couple of tissues from the pack, then when I take another look at his lip I pull a couple more.

"Just one is fine," he says.

He's wrong. I know this because of the two of us,

I'm the only one who's got a good look at what's on his lip. I pull out two or three more and then put the whole wad into his hand. I watch as his hand disappears inside his costume and reappears (with the tissues) inside the hood, right by his face. He dabs at his lip with the whole wad to take away the shine.

While he's wiping, I look around for anything other than his sweaty lip to lay my eyes on, and that's when I notice other kids pointing and staring at Hugo. At first I think it's for the usual reasons, and I am about to point back at them to see how they like it, but then I hear one kid say, "I wish I had a costume that good." Other kids say things like if they could be a fish ever in their life that's the kind of fish they'd want to be. Which is really something.

And that's when I get a pretty smart idea. I say to Hugo, "Have you made other costumes before?"

He says that he made all of his sisters' Halloween costumes last year, and why?

And I say, "We don't have to be good dancers to fix our problems."

"You said *we*, but I'm a pretty good dancer," Hugo says. "Like I've already said, it's you that's bad."

"Fine," I say. "I'm awful. The point is, what I am telling you now, is forget about the dancing. I think I just thought of another way to win."

17.

It's late and I'm supposed to be asleep with the light off and my drawing pad put away, missy. This is what my mom tells me after she's already been in my room twice to check on me. Mom says, "Penelope Rae." (Fractured spine.) "I'm not coming back in here again."

And she means it, I'm pretty sure. Because a little while later I can hear her snores all the way down the hall. Which sound like a goat unhappy about being chained to a fence.

I crumple a page from my drawing pad and toss it in the Heap in the center of my room.

Then I start on a new drawing.

If Leonardo da Vinci was here, he would surely say, "Dancing in a square, what craggy nonsense. I'd rather spend my time tasting what it's like to fly. But oh me, oh my, those shirt ruffles and bright skirts are quite appealing indeed."

I redraw the shirtsleeves on the boys' shirts again, and then I decide what they need is some color. On my way to the laundry room, which is where my mom keeps all of her art supplies, the snores cover my footsteps. Even so, I'm extra quiet when I pass Terrible's room, because it's late at night when aliens are the meanest.

I grab a mason jar of colored pencils from the top of the dryer, which Mom uses as a desk. The jar is behind stacks of her drawing books and watercolors of insides that look like stomachs, or else livers, I'm not sure which. On my way back, the goat isn't as loud as before for some reason, so I am extra careful not to step my bare tiptoes on any of the floorboards that squeak.

My brains must be concentrating too much on

where my feet are stepping, though, because I forget about what's in my hand, and the pencils clink against one side of the jar and then the other.

The snores go quiet. I go still. And when I do, I can hear Terrible's voice from his room. I get a chill all over and can't move, which is what usually happens just before an alien attack. All I can do is stare at his closed door and all of his DO NOT ENTER! PENELOPE, THIS MEANS YOU, WOMBAT signs, and wait. While I do, I happen to notice a new drawing taped to his door of a person being dangled out of a skyscraper window, and that person looks a lot like me, truth be told. I carefully remove one of the pencils from the jar and draw a safety net under the dangling me, you know, just in case. And while I do that, I hear his voice again, in between the goat.

I lean in closer and can't hear exactly what he's saying, but he's either talking in his sleep or he's on the phone. Even though it's past the time when we're allowed to be on the phone. (Aliens don't care very much for rules.)

Then I hear him say these words: "I can change."

Or maybe it's "I've got mange" or "Byron's on a plane." And then he says it again, louder this time. And it is "I can change." I'm pretty sure. He says some other things after that, but I can't make them out because for one thing, there's a door in the way. And for another, the goat across the hall is really getting going again.

I head back to my room in a hurry, wondering about Terrible, and if an alien can change, what will it change into? I stop when I notice the moon in the living room window. Tonight, from here, the moon looks different. The yellow is gone and is now pale gray, and I can almost make out a mouth that seems to say, "Even from here, you've got a long list of things to fix, Penelope Crumb. Better start singing."

So I do. I sing to the moon, real softly so nobody except me and the moon can hear.

I work on the drawings over the next week but I don't show them to Hugo. Not yet. He's an expert costume- and shoebox-maker, and I don't want him to say my drawings aren't any good. Just because

I'm a bad dancer doesn't mean I'm bad at everything. And I want Hugo to see the other side of the moon in me.

Grandpa says it's okay for Hugo to come along to one of his photography jobs as long as we understand that we're there to work and not to misbehave or create the type of problems that would cause him to lose his job or need an aspirin. He tells us this while we're on the way to the Portwaller Chamber of Commerce and doesn't let us out of the car until we say we understand.

Grandpa does a really good job of not staring at Hugo's sweaty lip just like I told him, and me and Hugo follow him from the parking garage down an alley into the Chamber. It's an old brick building with a wide window out front, and inside I can't help but notice how much it smells like coconut suntan oil. I mention this to Hugo, but after he gives the air a couple of hefty sniffs, he says he doesn't smell anything, not even a hint of coconut, which happens to be his favorite kind of pie.

But my nose has superpowers, this is what I tell

him, and I prove it when I spot three Tropic Breeze air fresheners hanging from the ceiling fan above the door.

"Pretty good," he says, staring at my big nose with what looks to me like a great deal of admiration.

Along the wood-paneled walls, there are shelves and shelves of brochures about what fun things to do in Portwaller, where to eat, where to buy stuff, and things like that. There are posters, too, with people who've got on smiles, fake ones with more gums and teeth than you ever would see in real life, the kind of smiles that are probably practiced over and over again until your cheek muscles get such a cramp and you forget what happiness really looks like anyway.

I guess those people in the posters are supposed to look just really lucky to be in Portwaller, doing whatever they are doing, but I've lived here my whole life and I've never seen anybody look like that. It's the kind of look that's called Unnatural. While Grandpa Felix talks to some lady about where to set up, I hold up one of Grandpa's cameras that I've got strung around my neck and I tell Hugo to smile like one of the people in the posters.

He turns away from the camera and tells me to cut it out. "I don't take good pictures," he says.

"Come on," I say, adjusting the focus.

He covers his face and says, "No, Penelope." And I think he means it.

I hand him Grandpa Felix's camera and say, "Here, you can take my picture." I go outside of the Chamber of Commerce and stand under the letters that spell out The City of Portwaller. Hugo follows, and when he says, "What are you doing?" I throw him the biggest smile I can, making all of my teeth and gums stick out in a way that I'm pretty sure makes me look demented.

This makes him laugh. He's got a low, rumbly laugh, Hugo does, one that I've never heard before. So I keep going. I put my hands in the air like they've just called my numbers for the Maryland Pick 3. Then I stretch my smile out even wider, like I want the moon to be able to see, until my cheeks start to pang.

Hugo is laughing so hard now that his whole body starts to shake and he doubles over. I drop my hands and put away my smile and worry that 1) he will keel over dead right here on the sidewalk; or 2) he will drop Grandpa Felix's expensive camera. Or both.

But to my surprise, he stands back up again and when he does he's smiling. Not crazy smiling like those people in the posters, or like I was doing, but smiling like a boy who's never been called Lippy Gordon, not for even one day. Before he can cover his face and tell me to stop, I pull the camera from his hands and start snapping, snapping. And what's more surprising is that he lets me.

18.

The next day, I decide to show my drawings to Hugo. I wait for him in the morning before school at the usual spot, and this time he doesn't wail when I jump out at him. "Look here," I say as I hand him my drawing pad.

"What's this?" he says.

I open it to the drawings I've been working on and say, "Mr. Sanders says each person gets points for dress attire, right?"

Hugo nods and then his eyes get big, really big.

"I think we could get enough points to win the

hoedown if we wear these costumes," I say, watching his face closely for a reaction.

"Where are we going to get costumes that look like this?" he asks.

I give him a look that says From You, Where Else?

He wipes his lip and then points to one of my drawings. "You want me to make these? For the whole square?"

"You can do it no problem," I tell him. "You are very good." Because when you are trying to get somebody to say yes to a lot of sewing, it helps to say nice things about their abilities. When he doesn't say yes right away, though, I add this: "I'll help."

Hugo leans in real close to the drawing, close enough for a drop of lip sweat to fall onto the page, right in the middle of the boys' shirt, and when he wipes it away, there's a smudge. He tells me he's sorry, about the sweat smudge, I'm guessing, and then he says, "What's that? It looks like a ruffle."

"That's because it *is* a ruffle," I say.

He shakes his head. "Ruffles."

"Are ruffles hard to make?" I ask.

"No, not really," he says, "but I just mean that, well . . . those are ruffles."

"You don't like ruffles?"

"On potato chips, sure."

I flip to the next page. "What about the skirt for the girls? Did you see how I put squares on it with everybody's initials?"

He sighs. "Yeah. You're a good artist, Penelope." Then he hands me back my drawing pad. "But . . ."

"What's wrong with them?" I want to know, because there is nothing wrong with them, not one thing.

"Nothing's wrong with them, exactly," he tells me. "It's just that, well, I don't think anybody is going to want to wear them."

I ask him why not and he says this: "Nancy Jo."

I hold up my drawing pad and say, "But these costumes would stand out a lot more than her white dresses and black shirts."

"Not everybody likes things that stand out," he says to me.

And I tell him that everybody should.

・ ・ ・

In gym class, the first thing I do is show everybody in our square.

Nancy Jo takes a look at my drawings and says, "What is this? I mean, really."

Then, when I explain that they are costumes, sort of like the ones from the square-dancing video that Mr. Sanders showed us, she says, "No. We've already decided what we are wearing. And my dad already bought me a new white dress."

Vera Bogg looks at my drawings and says, "Oooh, could they be pink?"

Vera Bogg knows that pink makes me feel like a sausage in a pickle jar. "No," I say, "they definitely could not be." Then I explain that we should have costumes to stand out at the hoedown, colorful ones, more than white dresses and black shirts. "We'll look more like a team, and we'll get more points."

Vera Bogg's partner, Nicholas, says, "That might work. I'm all for extra points."

Helena says, "The skirts *are* kind of pretty." And

then she glances sideways at Nancy Jo and takes a step backward like she expects poison darts to shoot out of Nancy Jo's nose and wants to get out of the line of fire.

I keep my eyeballs on Nancy Jo, and even though I've showed her a little bit of my other side with these drawings, she's got a look on her face that says You Are Awful, Penelope Crumb, Even Your Art Makes Me Sick. So I decide that maybe I need to show more of myself to her, you know, so she will change her mind, and I say, "Maybe the costumes will help make up for my bad dancing, too."

But seeing all of this must not be enough for Nancy Jo, she must need to see even more, because she grabs my drawing pad right out of my hands and begins flipping through the pages. "Wait a minute," she says. "I don't see any warts on these costumes. How can Wartgirl have a costume without any warts?"

I don't know where this comes from, but maybe when you've shown somebody all of your sides and they still don't like what they see, then maybe they don't deserve to see you in the first place, so I say this to Nancy Jo: "Yes, Nancy Jo. There will be lots of warts. So many you might want to fall out of a window."

Nancy Jo's mouth falls open. I hold out my hand and wait for her to return my drawing pad. She does, right away.

Hugo Gordon wipes his lip.

Helena says, "Huh? I don't get it."

I keep going, but this time, I'm not talking to Nancy Jo, I'm talking to everybody else. "Hugo is really good at making costumes and stuff. Did you see what he was for Be an Animal Day?"

"A whale?" says Nancy Jo, and she puffs out her cheeks and laughs.

Hugo finally says something. Finally. And this is what he says: "I was a fish."

Nancy Jo says, "Same thing."

"Not really," says Hugo. "A whale is a mammal, actually."

Nancy Jo folds her arms across her chest. "We are

not wearing any costume that looks like that. I've already got a new dress!"

I should stop right there, but I don't. I can't. I say to everyone except Nancy Jo, "Hugo can make anything. For real. You should see all the little people and furniture he's made for his shoebox houses."

As soon as I hear those words, the ones that I let go, I know what I've done. Hugo makes a terrible sound that comes from someplace deep inside him and when I look at him, he's got his head toward the floor and he might as well be staring at a plate of corn niblets.

I try to undo it. "What I meant was . . ."

But Nancy Jo is faster. "You mean like dolls?" she says. "For dollhouses?"

Nicholas laughs, and so does Helena and I don't know who else.

"No," I say, "they aren't dollhouses. I never said dollhouses." Then I look at Hugo. "I never said dollhouses," I tell him.

Hugo lifts his head and looks right at me then.

He's got a look on his face that says What Have You Done?

I want to say that I can fix this. I can. But the truth is, I don't know how.

He wipes his lip with the back of his arm. And then he walks out of gym class, just like that.

19.

I don't know whether to go after Hugo or if that will make things a thousand times worse, and while I'm trying to figure out what to do, Mr. Sanders says, "Okay, people, shall we get going?" And then he says, "Yes, let's. Up on your feet."

I get to my feet, but I'm not sure how I can get going anywhere without a partner. I keep looking at Mr. Sanders hoping that he notices Hugo's gone without me having to say it in front of everybody.

He doesn't. Instead he tells us that he's got some new songs to try out on us.

Good gravy.

The music starts, and I don't have a choice but to hold hands with nobody.

Vera Bogg says, "Tell Mr. Sanders that you don't have a partner, Penelope."

I shake my head. Besides, it's not like I've never danced with nobody before. After the bows, we circle right. Then the Caller in the song says promenade, and that's when the trouble begins. Somehow I end up outside the square again while everybody else keeps on dancing. This goes on for the rest of the song, and when the music finally stops, Mr. Sanders is right behind me.

"What's going on here?" he says. "It looks like we have a square breakdown."

Nancy Jo says, "She doesn't have a partner. Hugo's gone."

I throw her a look that says Which Was All Your Fault, and I am sure right then that there's no other side of the moon to Nancy Jo.

Mr. Sanders must think that *Hugo's gone* means that Hugo is home sick with the flu and not that he was here until a few minutes ago when I said something I didn't mean to. Because he says, "We're shy one partner here, huh? Well, that's not a problem. I can fill in."

There is only one thing worse in the world than square-dancing by yourself, and that's having to square-dance with your teacher. In front of every-body. Mr. Sanders makes an announcement, which makes me go dead. He says, real loud, "I'm going to be dancing with Penelope here, so the rest of you are on your own for this next song."

I know I am dead because I can't tell when Mr. Sanders takes my hands. I can't even feel my hands. And I can't hear the awful music. The room is spin-ning, spinning, and somehow I must get alive again because the next thing I know, Mr. Sanders is telling me to watch his feet, that I've stepped on them twice and he likes to keep his sneakers white. He smiles when he tells me this, but still.

Then I'm being dragged around the square, into the center and back, like a big-nosed mop, trying to keep up with Mr. Sanders, trying not to step on his white shoes, and trying not to think about what I did to Hugo.

It's just as bad as being called Wartgirl. And it's worse than actually having warts, I'm pretty sure.

When the dancing is finally over, Mr. Sanders gives me a long list of things I need to work on:

1. *Listen to the calls.*
2. *Follow your partner.*
3. *Shuffle your feet.*
4. *Step on the beat of the music.*
5. *Don't worry if you make a mistake, just keep on dancing.*

It's the last one that I'm having the most trouble with, I think.

After school, I wait for Hugo, figuring that maybe he went to see Mr. Fink in the sick room during gym. Which is where I would have liked to go. But I can't find him, and after a while I wonder if he went home.

Sitting by the frog wall, I draw the cracks in the bricks. There are even more new cracks and now the frog's got his head tucked under his leg because even he can't bear to look at me.

Grandpa Felix picks me up on time, and when I get in the car, he tells me we're going back to the bank for the reshoot. "I didn't bring Alfred this time," he says, "just the digitals. That should make them happy."

"Don't count on it," I say under my breath as I buckle myself in.

He taps the clock on the dashboard. "And at this moment we're right on time, so things are looking up."

As Grandpa Felix drives, he does a lot more talking than usual, and I don't know if that's because he's nervous about the bankers or because I'm being extra quiet worrying about Hugo. Talking hasn't worked out so good for me today, anyway, so I tell Grandpa not to worry and that I won't mess things up for him by accidentally telling the bankers stuff he doesn't want anybody to know like, for example, how he is afraid of hospitals because of the way they smell and also how he sometimes wears mismatched socks.

"I'm not worried about you messing things up,

little darling. You are just how I like you." Then he tugs at his right pant leg so I can see his sock. "And for your information, I've got on a matching pair today, blue stripes. So nothing to worry about. Plus I've been serenading the moon every night this week."

I shake my head and tell him that his singing-to-the-moon business is something I won't tell the bankers either.

We pull into the parking lot of the bank and Grandpa says, "Have you given it a try yet?"

"Once," I say.

"Did it help?"

"Not really."

"Once is no good. You've got to give it more than a once." Then he says, "Oh, I almost forgot. I developed the pictures from the other day at the Chamber of Commerce. There are a couple of your friend Hugo. I thought you might want to see them."

Grandpa Felix turns off the car and pulls out a couple of pictures from his satchel, black-and-white ones, of Hugo, the ones where he's smiling. He looks

like Hugo in all of them, he really does, but he sort of doesn't. And maybe it's because he's smiling, but you can't really see that much shine.

"What do you think?" says Grandpa.

I nod.

He musses my hair. "You are getting pretty good with the camera, you know."

"He looks different," I say. "In these pictures."

"Sometimes the camera has a way of seeing something the eye doesn't," he says. "Or can't." Then he grabs his camera bag from the backseat. "Ready to give this another try?"

I smile at him and tell him I am.

20.

Hugo isn't in gym the next day or the rest of the week. I don't see him in the cafeteria at lunch or before or after school by the frog cracks, either, and I look for him real good.

There's only one week until the hoedown and I've been singing to the moon every night. I sing all the songs about the moon that I can think of, even if I don't know all the words: the man in the moon, flying to the moon, swinging on a star, cow jumping over the moon, and walking in the moonlight. And even though it has nothing to do with the moon, I sing the glowworm song just because.

I don't know how all this singing is supposed to make me feel better like Grandpa said it would, but it doesn't, not at all. All it makes me feel is sore in the throat, and still, the moon won't show me anything else.

On Saturday morning, Littie Maple comes knocking. "Momma sent me over here so she could have some quiet time. That baby kept her up all night."

I tell her just wait until the baby gets here, then everybody will be up all night.

Littie says, "Mind if I watch TV?"

"There's no time for TV," I tell her. "I need your help."

I empty my piggy bank and my fake wallet on my desk. Then I ask Littie to lift up my mattress so I can get my real wallet.

"Your *real* wallet?" she says.

"The one that Terrible doesn't know about," I say. She lifts up one end of my mattress and I dive underneath it, grab my money, and crawl back out. She shakes her head and gives me a look that says You Are One Strange Bird. "If you ever have an alien for a brother, Littie Maple, and I hope you don't, but if you do, you'll do the same thing," I tell her. "Trust me."

I stuff all of my money into my pocket, grab my drawing pad, and Littie and me head out the door. Our first stop is TJ's Crafts a couple of blocks over. I lead Littie to the fabric department.

A lady behind the counter asks if she can help us. She's got orange hair that's cut short and looks very much like a helmet carved out of a pumpkin without the green stem on top. I catch Littie staring and have to poke her in the side with my elbow to make her quit.

I flip open my drawing pad and lay it on the metal counter in front of the lady. "I need some fabric to make these costumes, please."

She pulls a chair over to the counter and leans in close on her elbows to have a better look. While she does this, not one single hair on her head moves. She plays with the corner of the page, this lady does, curling the end and rolling it under her finger. "Okay," she says after a time. "What kind of fabric do you want?"

"I don't know," I tell her. "That's what I need

help with. How about orange?" I nudge the drawing pad with my thumb just enough to make her lose her grip on the rolled-up corner.

"Orange what?" she asks, whose name tag I now see says Welcome to TJ's, My Name Is Monica. She stands up quickly like she's not sure if I'm making fun of her hair or not. Which a lot of people must do, I'm pretty sure.

"Orange fabric?" And then I tell her how much I like the color orange for all the reasons that I do that have nothing at all to do with her pumpkin-helmet head.

Then Littie whispers to me, "I think she means what type of fabric and how much."

"Oh." I take all of my money out of my pocket and count it. "Forty-three dollars' worth of fabric."

"Excuse me for a moment," says Monica, and she pushes open a door behind her that says Employees Only.

"What do you think she's doing?" I ask Littie.

Littie shrugs. "Maybe that's where they keep all of the orange fabric."

There are rolls of fabric standing on end against round tables nearby. While we wait for Monica, Littie and me start looking. Littie finds some that looks like teddy bear fur. She rubs it against her cheek. "I wish I knew how to sew. I'd make a bear or something for the new baby."

I find a shiny gold one that looks like somebody's poured a billion stars into it. "That probably costs a lot more than forty-three dollars."

While we're looking, another lady, an older one, comes to the counter then and says, "Pardon me, young ladies, how can I help you?" Her name tag says her name is Dolores, and underneath her name, it says Textile Supervisor.

I show Dolores my drawings and tell her the same thing I told Monica before she disappeared behind that door. She smiles, this lady does, and she says she has something she thinks will do the trick. Dolores goes across the room gathering up rolls of fabric in her arms and then lays them on the counter in front of us.

She unfolds one roll of red cloth, and when she

does, I know that it's perfect. Even though it's not orange. "What do you think about something like this?" she says.

"There are tiny dancers on it," says Littie. "In Western outfits."

Dolores holds up some other fabric, too, blue denim, and says we can use some of this for the trim on the skirt. Then she says, "How many costumes are you planning on making?"

"Just two," I say.

When we're all done at TJ's, Littie and me get on the metro headed north. It's crowded because it's Saturday, so we have to stand near the door.

"Hugo doesn't know you're coming over," says Littie.

I tuck the bag of fabric along with my drawing pad under my arm. "Nope."

"And you don't know if he's going to make the costumes or if he's even going to want to be your partner or go to the hoedown," she says.

"Nope," I say. "Nope. Nope."

Littie scoots closer to me when we stop at the next station so that people can get off the train. "That's a lot of nopes. I'm just saying."

"I have to try, Littie Maple. I have to." Then I take her hand and sing, *"Bow to your lady, bow to your gent, follow your lady left, that's the way she went."* I take her around in a circle, trying not to bump into anybody else on the train. *"Into the center now, tall and grand, come back and promenade all around the land."* I take her into the center of the train and then spin her around and around, which I know is not really a promenade, but it's the best I can do with what I've got.

It's a short walk from the metro stop to Hugo's building. As we go up to the seventh floor in the elevator, I warn Littie about his sisters and tell her she should be fine because she isn't wearing any rubber bands in her hair.

We stand in front of Hugo's door for a while. For one thing, I'm not 100 percent sure that this is the right door. And for another, what if he tells me he can't stand the sight of me or the red square-dancing fabric and starts cutting it up into small pieces right in front of me. It could happen, I'm pretty sure.

"What are you doing?" asks Littie.

"Nothing."

"Exactly," she says. "Aren't you supposed to be knocking? I'm just saying."

"Okay, I'm doing it," I say. "Don't rush me." And then as I raise my fist to knock, I say, "I hope this is the right apartment."

"What?" says Littie, taking a step back.

Marta or Veronica, one of them, I can't tell which one, answers the door. "Hey, it's Hugo's friend," she says. Then she looks at Littie. "With another friend."

I say hi and then ask if Hugo is home.

"Nope," she says. "Not at home."

"Oh." I look at Littie. "Do you know when he'll be back? Because maybe we could wait around?"

Littie's eyes get wide like this wasn't part of the deal. But then Marta or Veronica, whichever sister this is, says, "Sorry, no can do. But I will tell him you stopped over whenever I see him again." She starts to close the door.

"Wait!" I open my drawing pad and tear out the page of my drawings. Then I stick it in the bag with the fabric and hand it to her. "Can you give him this?"

"What's it for?"

"It's for Hugo," I say. "He'll know."

21.

There's only one week until the hoedown and Mr. Sanders pulls me aside before gym and tells me he's been trying to find me a new partner.

"What about Hugo?" I say. "Hugo's my partner. I don't need a new one."

Mr. Sanders cocks his head to one side. "Didn't I tell you? I thought for sure that I had. I received a note from Hugo's mother and he is being excused from gym."

"I don't understand," I say. Because I don't.

"He had a note," says Mr. Sanders. Which I guess explains it all. "Anyway, if I can't get you another partner in time, I'll dance with you at the hoe-down."

Good gravy.

After school, I finally see Hugo walking out the side door by the cafeteria. Which I imagine he's doing to hide from me. I have to run to catch up with him, and when I do, he jumps. And gives a holler.

"Where have you been?" I say.

"Why do you always do that?" he says.

"Do what?"

He keeps on walking. "Never mind."

"Were you sick?" I ask.

"Something like that."

"Are you better?" I say.

He shrugs, and cuts through the playground.

I tell him that Littie and me stopped by and dropped off the drawings and the fabric with his sister and did he get them?

"Yeah," he says. "I got them."

"So what do you think?"

"You should see if you can return it," he says. "And get your money back."

My mouth gets dry and I have to swallow a couple of times before I can say, "Why?"

"Because I'm not your partner anymore, Penelope," he says. "I'm not dancing in the hoedown, I'm not going back to gym, and I'm not making any costume." That's a lot of nots, I notice, and by the last one his face is really red.

"I'm really sorry," I say. "I was only trying to tell them, to make them understand how good you are. So they could see the other side of you. I didn't mean to tell them about your shoebox houses or whatever you call them, but I just wanted them to see."

"Well, now they do," he says. "They see a fat kid with a sweaty lip who plays with dolls. So, thanks a lot." He starts off.

"No, wait," I say, grabbing his arm. I reach into my backpack and pull out the pictures I took of him. "These are for you."

He glances at them but keeps his distance. "What are they?"

I push them at him and don't stop until he takes them in his hands. When he finally does, he looks them over and then tries to give them back. "They're for you," I tell him again.

He grunts something that might be "thanks" but I don't know. And then he walks past the basketball court toward Record Street.

I let him go. "If it makes you feel better," I shout when he reaches the hoop, "I have to dance with Mr. Sanders at the hoedown!"

He keeps on walking, but turns his head and says, "A little." I'm pretty sure.

"You look very nice," Mom tells me when I finally come out of my room.

I've got on a white skirt that has tiny blue flowers on it, and white top with a Peter Pan collar that doesn't look very hoedown-y, but truth be told, I'm not in a very hoedown-y mood.

"Are you sure you can't write me a note?" I say. "I mean, I have to dance with Mr. Sanders in front of all those people. Don't you think that deserves a note? Because I do."

"She's got a point," says Terrible. "I mean, people

already think she's weird, and now she's going to be known forever as the girl who square-danced with the gym teacher."

"People don't think she's weird," says Mom, smoothing the hair in my ponytail.

"Yes they do," me and Terrible say at exactly the same time. "Lately, anyway," I add.

Mom says, "Penelope Rae." (Tonsillitis.)

"It's okay," I tell her. "That's just one side of me."

Grandpa Felix is downstairs waiting for us in his car. "Don't say I look nice," I say when I climb in the backseat.

"I wasn't going to," he says. "I was going to say you look lovely."

Then he looks at my mom, and I can hear her whisper, "Don't ask."

"Did you hear back from the bank people?" I ask when Grandpa pulls away from our building.

"I did indeed."

"Well?" I say. "Did they like the pictures?"

"I'm very pleased to report that they did," he says. "Very much, in fact. It seems as though all that singing has paid off." As Grandpa drives us down the street, he points at the windshield. "Did you see that moon?"

I keep my eyes on the streetlights and the buildings we pass. Anywhere but the moon.

"It's full tonight," he says. "That lantern moon. Did you see that, Penelope?"

"No," I say. "I didn't. But even if I did, it's not like we can see the whole thing, anyway. Not if the rest wants to stay in the dark."

"What are you two talking about?" says Mom.

"See," says Terrible, from beside me. "Weird."

22.

The parking lot is full, and when I see all those cars, all those people who will be watching, I look at my hands. For the first time, I really feel like a Wartgirl, even without the warts.

Patsy Cline and Vera Bogg are waiting for me out front, and we go inside together. Patsy is in one of her country-western singing outfits, a green one with fringes and a matching cowgirl hat. Vera Bogg is in a pink dress with pink shoes and a pink bow in her hair that I know she would dye pink, too, if she could find a way.

"What happened to wearing a white dress?" I ask Vera.

She shrugs. "I don't have one, and I just figured I'd dance a lot better if I was comfortable, and I happen to be most comfortable in pink."

"What will Nancy Jo say?" I ask with a smile.

Vera beams. "She's already started calling me Pinky Bogg. And I've always wanted a nickname."

Patsy Cline is chewing on her thumb and looks like she's concentrating hard. She says, "Quick, what's the allemande again? I forget."

Pinky Bogg says it's when you turn halfway, then let go hands and step forward. "Or is that shucking the corn?"

"You're lucky," Patsy Cline says to me. "You have Mr. Sanders right there if you forget how to do a call."

I give Patsy a look that says Did You Ship Your Brains to Outer Space?

And then she laughs, and so does Pinky. Which starts me going, and it feels good to see the funny side of things, even if that side is really, really small.

Patsy Cline stops laughing all of a sudden, and her eyes get real big like she's just seen something with a tail and is going into an allergic shock. Before I have a chance to ask her if she needs help, there's a tap on my shoulder. I turn around.

"Wartgirl," says Hugo Gordon after he wipes his lip. But I barely notice the shine or what he called me because he is wearing a red shirt with tiny square dancers on it, just like the one I drew.

I don't know what to say, so what comes out is this: "Hello there, Lippy Gordon. Nice shirt."

He laughs. "This is for you." And he hands me my wide skirt with ruffles.

I hold it up. It's just like my drawing except for the brown dots on the ruffles. "What are these?" I say.

"Warts. What else?" Then he turns around so I can see the back of his shirt. Across the back, just below the collar in black letters is LIPPY.

The microphone from inside the gym squeals, and Patsy Cline says, "Come on, we've got to get going." I tell them I'll meet them inside, but I have to go to the bathroom and change into my skirt.

The bathroom is empty all except for someone in

a stall who is busy doing I don't know what, but I can hear the toilet paper roll spinning and spinning. I'm pretty sure. I quick slide out of my white skirt with blue flowers and pull on my wide red skirt with warty ruffles. I give it a whirl and out it goes, just like the ladies in the square-dancing video. If Mister Leonardo da Vinci was here, he would surely say, "There is nothing better, oh me, oh my, than art that comes to life."

While I'm whirling, the door to the stall opens and there standing in front of me in a new white dress that her dad bought for her is Nancy Jo.

Good gravy.

She looks almost as surprised to see me as I am to see her. And that's when I notice the huge purple stain on her dress. Because let me tell you it's real noticeable.

"That's a nice dress," I say. Which is the truth because it looks like it was very nice before some giant purple space creature threw up all over it.

Nancy Jo has a wad of toilet paper in her hand,

and she's wiping furiously at the stain. Which is making it worse, truth be told.

"It's grape juice," she says, her eyes filling up with tears. "My dad is going to kill me. He told me to be careful. But I was thirsty. He's going to kill me, he is."

I tell her that I know a thing or two about dead things and that I'm pretty sure no one has ever died from a grape juice stain on a dress.

"No, you don't understand," she tells me. "He will be so mad."

I hand her a paper towel to wipe her eyes, but she wets it under the sink and gets back to scrubbing at the stain. After a time, she sinks to the floor. "It's not going to come out, is it?"

"I don't think so," I tell her. Because that's the truth. But the truth isn't always easy to take, because Nancy Jo keeps on scrubbing. I can't understand why her dad or anybody would get so worked up about a stain, because, my word, if my mom was this concerned about stains on clothes I would've been dead a long time ago.

· · ·

And then for the first time in the middle of the girls' bathroom at Portwaller Elementary, I think I finally see the other side of Nancy Jo as she sits here wringing the fabric on her dress and trying so hard to get rid of that spot so nobody will see, so nobody else will find out. And while she sits there, I see that maybe, just maybe, this girl knows deep down inside what it's like to be called a name or what it's like to have a sweaty lip.

Maybe we do get to see more than one side of the moon, once in a while, if we just look hard enough. And when that happens, you have to do something, you have to offer a girl your white flowered skirt, for example, if she wants it.

She does.

Nancy Jo wipes her eyes and thanks me.

I take one last look in the bathroom mirror, which I don't like to do very much because the world is full of other things to look at, thank lucky stars. But when I do, I am glad, so glad, to see all sides of me.

23

Me and Hugo are holding hands. We stand in our square while Mr. Sanders takes the microphone and welcomes the guests to the hoedown. I watch them all file into the gym past dried cornstalks in big bunches by the door, past the hay stacked five bales high along the walls.

They fill up the bleachers pretty quick, under rows of hollowed-out gourds strung together with twinkle lights. Everything looks so barn-y and nice, including me and Hugo in our costumes, that for a time I can almost forget we are about to do a square-dance contest in front of a whole bunch of people and I can almost forget that I'm awful at it. Almost.

Mr. Sanders says to everyone sitting in the bleachers, "Before we begin, should I explain how the scoring works? I think that's probably a good idea. Well, squares will be scored on synchronicity and timing, but each dancer can earn points for how they are dressed and their attitude." He flashes a smile to the crowd. "Those with the most points are going to opening day of Simmons's newest fun park, Adventureland."

Lots of people hoot and clap, and I can hear Angus Meeker shout, "Spin Rocket first in line!"

Nancy Jo glances at the bleachers and then back at my flowered skirt, the one she has over her dress.

Mr. Sanders says, "Now, let me introduce our distinguished judges." He points to a table in front of the bleachers. "Our three judges for tonight's hoedown are Vice Principal Hardy, my sweet wife, Mrs. Georgia Brown-Sanders, and fourth-grade teacher Miss Stunkel."

My word. Miss Stunkel is a judge. She's the whole

way across the room but she's got her chicken-bone finger out and she's pointing it in my direction, I'm pretty sure.

Everybody claps, and Mr. Sanders waits until they're done to say, "Now that we've got all that out of the way, should we start the hoedown? Yes indeed. Let's square-dance!"

Hugo wipes his lip and squeezes my hand tight like he's worried I might get the urge to run as fast as I can out the door and hide with one of the cracks in the five-legged frog, or worse, that he will. I squeeze back to let him know I'm not going anywhere.

Vera Bogg and everybody else in our square look like they've eaten potato salad that's spent too much time in the hot sun. Especially Nancy Jo, who so far hasn't said anything about how much she really, really wants to win this prize so don't mess up, Wartgirl. She hasn't said anything at all, in fact. She just fidgets in place, shifting from one foot to the other, and pulling at the white lacy collar at her neck. We're all being too quiet, which doesn't help the nerves, and I really wish somebody would say something.

Finally, Nancy Jo says this: "Penelope, say something about dead things, would you?"

I say, "What?" Because I'm not sure I heard her right.

"Talk about dead things," she says. "Please."

I'm so happy I could almost die. I mean, for one thing, she called me Penelope. And for another, I've been wanting to share this one for a long time: "Just before Thomas Edison died, they put his last breath into a bottle," I say.

Nicholas: "No way."

Me: "True blue."

Nancy Jo: "What did they do with it? I mean, really."

Vera Bogg: "For perfume?"

Me: "It's probably in a museum somewhere."

Hugo: "Or maybe NASA is doing some experiments with it."

Helena: "Creepy."

Nicholas: "No. It's at the Smithsonian Museum or something."

Then Nancy Jo says this: "No, Nicholas, I bet

Hugo's right. NASA is doing something with it."
She really does.

I say, "Yeah, but if they ever open that bottle, I bet that breath really stinks."

Hugo starts laughing and then pretty soon our whole square is breaking up about it. By the time Mr. Sanders starts the music I'm feeling a lot better and wonder why square dancing can't just be like this without the dancing part.

I try to listen to the calls, I really do, and for the most part, with some helpful whispers from Hugo and occasionally even Nancy Jo, my feet go in almost all the right places, thank lucky stars. Our square stays in a square the whole time, except when we're circling or making a star, and never falls apart into a clump, not even once.

When the last song comes to an end, there's a lot of clapping, even from Miss Stunkel, I notice. While the judges are scribbling on pieces of paper about how good we are or aren't, I tell Hugo that I'm sorry I stepped on his foot twice during a promenade but isn't twice a lot better than my usual five and isn't that the sort of thing that's called Improvement?

Hugo says, "Don't worry, I stuffed the toes of my shoes with cotton, so I didn't feel a thing."

Helena says that her mom and dad are taking her to Itzy's Pizza after the hoedown and does everybody else want to come? Everybody else in our square says they do because Itzy's is ten times better than Maggie's Italian Restaurant plus they have an arcade next to the bathroom. Nancy Jo says Itzy's is her favorite and then adds, "I mean, I hope I can go, if my dad says it's okay."

I don't say anything, and neither does Hugo, because I don't know if they mean us. I don't know if, to them, Hugo and me are *everybody*. But then Nancy Jo says, "Penelope and Hugo, do you want to come?"

Hugo smiles like one of the people in the posters at the Portwaller Chamber of Commerce, gums and all. And before I can say, "Welcome to Portwaller!" Mr. Sanders gets back on the microphone and says, "Ladies and gentlemen, our judges have picked our winners."

Then he takes a piece of paper in his hands, unfolds it real slowly, like it's the answer that solves an ancient riddle, and maybe it is, maybe it could be. Everybody, and I mean everybody, in our square holds hands. I squeeze my eyes shut.

Mr. Sanders calls out the winning square first. It's not us.

I open my eyes. Angus Meeker and his square, when hearing Mr. Sanders call their names, start hooting and jumping and high-fiving all over the place.

Nancy Jo looks at me, and I worry that she's going to say I'm the reason we didn't win after all, and that she'll also say I'll be Wartgirl Forever no matter how hard I try not to be, but she doesn't. She just shrugs and says, "Spin Rocket will still be there the day after opening day, you know."

I'm still in a bit of a shock from what Nancy Jo didn't say, so I don't hear Mr. Sanders call the name of the kid who won for Best Attitude. It's a fifth-grade boy, whose name I don't know, two squares over, and he's waving to his family in the bleachers with both hands.

Then Mr. Sanders says, "And finally, the winner for Best Attire." He holds the piece of paper with judges' scribbles close to his nose and then drops his hand to his side. He looks at the judges. "My gracious, do we have a tie?" The judges nod, all three of them. Then Mr. Sanders says, "Indeed, it seems we do have a tie. How do you like that?" He looks at the paper once again. "The winners are Bart Miller and Patsy Cline Watson."

Right away, Patsy Cline takes off her green cowgirl hat and waves it to the cheering crowd. Her partner, Bart, adjusts his green jacket with white fringe along the sleeves and takes a bow. Then Mr. Sanders says, "And also Hugo Gordon and Penelope Crumb. Let's give all our winners a hearty round of applause. The winners and their squares will be treated to coupons for a free ice cream, courtesy of Marauder's Treat Shop."

Vera Bogg says, "Free ice cream, yum!" and Nicholas and Helena's partner high-five. Me and Hugo just stand there dumbstruck. The whole gym is clapping for us, I mean *really* clapping for us, for

Lippy Gordon, for Wartgirl, and for who knows why else.

Hugo takes my hand and swings it. And real quick, before the clapping stops and this is all over, I grab his other hand. He gives me a look that says What Now? but there's no time to answer. Instead, we promenade around the whole floor of the gym, past the bales of hay, past the rest of the squares and the crowds in the bleachers, so that everyone has a chance to really see us.

"Where are we going?" Hugo asks as we promenade between the dried cornstalks and out the gymnasium door.

"Out here," I tell him, and we don't stop until I can feel the night air on my nose, until we're standing in the light of that lantern moon.

Hugo wipes his lip. "What are you staring at?" he asks, looking up.

The moon, bright white now, slips behind a cloud. Still not wanting us to see. "Just checking for fur-covered fish people," I say.

"See any?"

I shake my head. "Not yet. But they're up there. I'm pretty sure." Hugo doesn't say I'm wrong, and maybe it's because he knows now, too. I look up awhile longer, until my neck starts to cramp, and then I say, "Come on, let's go eat pizza. Our square's waiting for us."

Be sure to pick up all the books in the
PENELOPE CRUMB series!

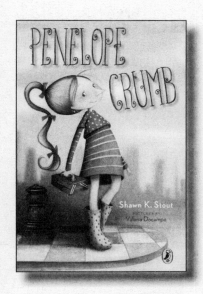

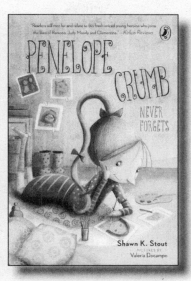